LOVE and
Lemongrass

Books by Shannon Page

Eel River
Our Lady of the Islands (with Jay Lake)
I Was a Trophy Wife (essay collection)

The Nightcraft Quartet:
The Queen and The Tower
A Sword in The Sun
The Lovers Three
The Empress and The Moon

Island of Second Chances:
A Taste of Midnight
Love and Lemongrass
The Touch of Silk (forthcoming)

Collaborations, as Laura Gayle

The Chameleon Chronicles:
Orcas Intrigue
Orcas Intruder
Orcas Investigation
Orcas Illusion
Orcas Intermission

Tales from the Berry Farm:
Orcas Afterlife
Orcas Aliens (forthcoming)

LOVE and *Lemongrass*

BOOK TWO
ISLAND OF SECOND CHANCES

SHANNON PAGE

ALøT
PRESS
A Little of This, Inc.

HUMAN AUTHORED™
AG THE Authors Guild
9792314

First Edition

ISBN: 978-1-967168-03-3

ALOT PRESS
A Little of This, Inc.

"Darling, do consider the more local delights, the tasty treats from near at hand—a neighboring farmer's field, the village bakeshop, the pillow beside your own."

—Countess Lucinda Devonryshireton,
The Countess's Exceedingly Perfect Guide to Love and Romance, Volume IV

Chapter 1

STEPH

Twenty-nine years ago

There he was again. The cute blond fellow that Steph had seen at least a dozen times already, at the dim sum place where she regularly picked up a Combo Box Number Six to eat in the park on her all-too-brief lunch hour.

They'd noticed each other the first time, smiled tentatively at each other the second time, said "Hi" the third time, and then… that's where it had stalled out. Just another "Hi" each time.

Steph had had quite enough of this, she'd finally decided last week. She was going to break the impasse, take matters into her own hands. Frustratingly, since she'd made this resolution, he hadn't turned up.

But here he was! Walking in as she was leaving with her lunch, just as cute as ever, and smiling shyly at her like he did every single time…

"Hi!" she said, clutching her Combo Box. "Great to see you again!"

"Uh, yeah, hi," he mumbled, still smiling but now glancing down at his feet. He moved to step around her on his way to the counter.

Steph moved just enough to block his route as another customer came in and walked around them both. The cute blond guy looked up at her, clearly confused. At a loss. "Uh," he said again.

"Sorry!" Steph said, grinning widely, conveying, she hoped, a complete lack of sorrow. "But I made myself a promise, and I'm not one to go back on promises. To anyone."

The man blinked at her. "You're not?"

"Nope, I'm not," she said quickly, not letting herself lose her stride even though when she'd planned this all out and rehearsed it in her imagination, he was supposed to say *What was the promise?* She forged ahead. "I promised myself that the next time I saw you, I'd introduce myself." She held out the hand not holding her lunch. "I'm Steph Hancock."

He stared at her hand for an uncomfortably long moment before producing his own. "David Palmer."

She took his hand and shook it warmly but firmly. While still holding onto it, she said, "Nice to meet you, David. I'm about to go eat my lunch in the park across the street. It's such a pretty day. Would you like to join me?"

Now he looked panicked, and she felt him trying to pull his hand away. She let it go but amped up her smile, and didn't move out of his way. "I. Um. Usually take it back to the office?" he finally squeaked out.

"Where do you work?"

"Smith Barney. The brokerage house?"

She nodded. "That's not far from my office. Do you actually have to go right back, or can you take a few minutes?"

"I...suppose I could take a few minutes." He looked less panicked now, but more confused. "Why?"

For crying out loud, do I have to spell it out? "Because we see each other here all the time, and we nod and say hi, and I'd like to get to know you better." She gave him another hopeful smile. "I'm not a serial killer, I promise."

His eyes widened. They were light blue, almost sky-colored: gorgeous. "I didn't think you were a serial killer! You're too—" And then he clamped his mouth shut as his cheeks colored.

"I'm too what?" Steph asked sweetly. *Pretty? He was going to say I'm pretty!*

Maybe?

"Uh, too…female," he stammered. "Serial killers are almost exclusively male."

Steph snorted with laughter. "Oh, so you did notice!"

His cheeks reddened further, and more customers kept filtering into the tiny takeout joint; now a line was forming at the counter.

"Get your lunch," Steph went on, finally moving out of his way. "I'll wait here, and we can walk over to the park together."

"Okay," he said, and gave her another fragile smile.

After a minute, Steph stepped outside to wait on the sidewalk. It was getting very crowded in there, and noisy as well. Besides, this was the only door. It wasn't as though David could slip out the back and flee from her.

Even though I'm totally not a serial killer, she told herself.

Once he'd emerged and they'd settled on her favorite park bench, Steph opened her box of dim sum and pulled out the pork bun. "Mmm," she said, around a fluffy mouthful. "Perfect as ever."

He had gotten a different combo; number fourteen, she thought. Heavy on the seafood. "Yes," he agreed. "They do a good job there."

She snapped her bamboo chopsticks apart and picked up a siu mai dumpling, popping it in her mouth. "I have friends up in the city who say Yank Sing is the best, but frankly, I've never been as impressed with them as I am with this little hole-in-the-wall down here." She grinned over at him. "Or maybe it's just because I can walk here from my office, and familiarity breeds contentment."

He looked briefly confused, then laughed. "Oh! That's funny."

"Thank you." Okay, this was all still fairly awkward, but at least she'd made him laugh.

"Where do you work?" he asked.

She wanted to cheer: the man asked a question! He was showing interest! "A-1 Insurance, just over there." She pointed across the street with a chopstick. "The most boring job in the history of the world, and I'm happy to have it. Not many jobs out here for English majors, I'm afraid."

"You're an English major?" His confused look was back.

"Was. Graduated from Stanford last year, and couldn't find a single company that was looking for someone who could analyze a Victorian novel and delineate its themes, or even diagram a sentence. And before you ask, no, they don't make you diagram sentences in college—though I could do it in a heartbeat if anyone needed me to. Fifty cents a sentence, or three for a dollar." She gave him a hopeful smile, then added, "That was another joke. You could laugh again if you wanted to." *You're even cuter when you laugh.*

To her surprise, he did laugh. "You're a very interesting person, Steph."

"Thanks!" She ate another siu mai. It was the combination of the ground pork and ground shrimp that made it, she thought, already wondering if she could learn how to make them herself. "So what do you do at Smith Barney? Are you a broker?"

Those blue eyes widened. "Oh no. An analyst. I…uh…they don't let me talk to the customers."

"They don't?"

He smiled broadly. It was like the sun had come out after a cloudy morning. "That was a joke too. But it's also true. I'm a little, uh, shy."

"You know? I had actually noticed that," she said, gently.

His smile turned wry. "Most people do."

Ouch. So she eased off then, asking him more questions, but easy ones, nothing too intrusive, and offered little tidbits of information about herself. When they'd both finished their boxes, he started to seem nervous again, glancing over at the tall building where his office was. So she made sure to exchange numbers, both home and cell.

Well, her cell number. He didn't have one. "I don't, um, talk on the phone much. Nobody needs to reach me—well, I'm usually either at work or at home, so it didn't seem important to get yet another line."

"Fair," she said. "So, what do you say: lunch next Tuesday? Same place, same time?"

"I'd like that," he said, with no stammer at all.

Fifteen years ago

"ARE YOU DISAPPOINTED?"

Steph reached across the table and took David's hand. He squeezed hers, and she squeezed back as a few tears leaked out of her eyes. "Yes. No. I don't know." She shook her head and said again, "I don't know. Are you?"

He exhaled a soft sigh. "I think I'm 'yes and no and I don't know' as well."

"It would have changed so much."

"It would have."

The waitress came to their table. Steph asked for a coffee, with plenty of cream; David asked for the same, and a plate of strawberry mini-muffins to share. She jotted their order down and stepped quickly away. Steph wondered if she saw lots of couples like this, in here. So close to the clinic as it was.

"But I think I was ready for such a change," Steph said. "I mean, I wasn't, when we thought the decision had been made for us. But after my initial freakout…"

David gave her a kind smile, a loving smile. "*Our* initial freakout."

"Oh, you didn't panic half as much as I did."

"Well, I've always been quieter than you," he teased.

She smiled back at him and wiped away a tear with the hand he wasn't holding.

The waitress came back with their coffees. "Your muffins will be along in a minute."

After she left again, Steph ventured, "Well. We could always adopt."

"We could. Do you want to?"

"Yes. No. I don't know." She stirred cream into her coffee and took a sip. At least she wouldn't ever have to give up caffeine, even temporarily. Or brie, or sushi. Or wine! There was always a bright side, if you just took the time to look for it. "We could look into it. But there's no rush."

"There is no rush," he agreed. "But we could, when you're ready—look into it, I mean. Or I would be happy to do the research, and let you know what I find out. When you're ready."

"Thank you." She took a deep breath, and another sip of coffee.

The waitress brought the mini-muffins. Steph took a long time tearing one apart, dabbing butter on its still-steaming interior, letting it melt, taking a bite. Her mind deconstructed the recipe almost automatically. It would have been so much fun to teach her child how to cook, how to bake. To share all her kitchen insights, her love of flavors, her appreciation for food made by others and her delight in making it herself.

But would her child have been interested? You never knew, did you? Steph's mother had not been able to interest her, or her brother or sister, in her own hobby of heirloom rose cultivation. Steph enjoyed gardening, of course, but exclusively edible plants. Gardening was a means to an end, and the end was cooking.

Cooking had been Steph's passion for as long as she could remember. From the earliest days when her mom had let her sit on the kitchen counter beside the stove, stirring the Campbell's chicken noodle soup as it heated up; through when she had followed her first recipe to make something from scratch (grilled cheese sandwiches with tomato jam), when she could barely read; until her first invented meal, in junior high: a riff on her mom's meatloaf, making it spicier, and also into meatballs, which she served over pasta with a homemade sauce at the family's Sunday dinner. Only after everyone had remarked on how delicious it was had her mom told everyone that Steph had created the dish herself, with no help.

Cooking still gave Steph's life its richness, its delight. It was her creative outlet. David worked long hours, now at a smaller, more specialized brokerage firm, and still as an analyst. Steph still worked in insurance administration. It was tedious and re-petitive, but it paid well, she was good at it, and when she left the office at five o'clock sharp every day, she never had to give her work a thought until the next morning.

When she'd missed a period, thirty-six-year-old Steph had looked at thirty-seven-year-old David and said, "We need to talk about something important."

When the period showed up two weeks late, they were already well on their way to wrapping their hearts and minds around the idea of having a child. Though they'd been married nearly twelve years, it had always seemed too soon…there was always time to think about it…later.

Suddenly, later was now. So, without fully committing one way or another, Steph went off birth control, and they agreed to see what happened.

What happened was more irregular periods, weight gain, and a year of doctor's visits and tests…and finally, almost an hour ago, a diagnosis of late-onset PCOS—polycystic ovary syndrome. Steph was not technically infertile—miracles did happen—but the doctor advised that it would be best if they assumed that she was. She'd offered Steph and David a referral to an IVF clinic.

They'd taken the clinic's pamphlet, but Steph had asked the doctor to hold off on the formal referral. "For now," she said. "I just need to absorb this for a while."

The doctor smiled at them both, her face filled with empathy and care. "I understand. I'm here if you need me—for anything."

"Thank you."

Now Steph looked at David across the table. "You're not eating any muffins," she said.

His smile, even his sad smile, was still like the sun coming out. "I'm really not all that hungry."

"You know, I'll never understand that." She gave him a watery smile back, and tried not to think about what their child might have looked like.

Nine years ago

DAVID WAS ON the couch when she got home from work. Wrapped up in a blanket, staring at the television, which was tuned to a game show, with the sound off. He was shivering.

Steph set her purse on the entry table and sat on the other end of the sofa. David didn't look at her, but from this angle, she could see he wasn't really looking at the TV either.

He was just staring. At nothing. At the abyss. At his darkness, somewhere in the middle distance, where it seemed no one could reach.

And still shivering, though the room was overly warm.

Eventually, she got up, went into the kitchen, and returned with a mug of hot chocolate. She set it on the coffee table in front of him. His gaze flickered; he seemed to just now register her presence.

"Rough day?" she asked, softly.

He nodded.

"Did you talk to your boss again?"

He shook his head.

Steph forced back her frustration, schooled her emotions. Calm, peaceful, unchallenging. "It's bad for the whole team, if they let certain members get away with bullying. Because that's what it is: bullying."

He shrugged.

"You're by far the most valuable member—not just of the team, but of the whole damn brokerage house. I hope they know they're going to lose you if they can't get this under control."

Now he turned and blinked at her. "I can't quit this job," he whispered. "We need it."

"We actually don't," she said quietly. Calmly. "We enjoy the money, but we're doing fine. We would be fine if you didn't work for a year. We would be fine if you got a nice relaxing job that paid half the money." She nodded at the mug before him. "Drink your cocoa."

He picked up the mug and took a sip. Then he set the mug back on the table.

Steph looked at the TV. The game show contestants were very excited about something, hopping up and down. Maybe the hopping was part of the game? She didn't understand what the contest was, but the colors—of the studio set, of the contestants' clothing, of the host's clothing—were certainly very bright.

Was it a Japanese game show?

She turned back to David, who had relaxed slightly, and had stopped shivering. After another long moment, he picked up the mug and took another sip. This time, he held onto the mug, and continued sipping.

Steph let out a breath. He was talking (well, whispering), and drinking his hot chocolate: they'd gotten around the edge of this one. Probably.

When he finished the mug and set it back on the coffee table, she said, "I'm going to go start on dinner. Are you going to be okay in here for a while?"

He turned and gave her a ghost of a smile. "Yes. Thank you." And then, "I'm sorry."

She slowly reached out a gentle hand and touched his arm.

"No need to be sorry. You're safe, and I love you."

"I love you too."

In the kitchen, she took a few more deep, centering breaths, and wondered whether to call his therapist tomorrow. He'd been doing so much better, for so long…but they kept coming back to this.

Workplaces were supposed to be accommodating, both by law and just because of simple human decency. Harassment, of course, was not supposed to be tolerated at all. That was the theory, anyway.

There was a certain breed of dude-bro-asshole brokers, she'd learned. And that breed, like dogs that bite no matter what, just had to bully people. Even the analyst upon whom they relied for the information they needed to actually, you know, serve their clients and be successful in their business. Why would they do that? Steph would never understand such people.

Not that this job, or any job, had caused David's issues in the first place. No, the responsibility for that lay squarely with his parents.

She poured herself a half-glass of wine and stared into the fridge, part of her mind figuring out what to make for dinner while the rest of her pondered how to fix this. Not how to fix David—only he could do that, to whatever degree was even possible—but what she could do to make their situation better.

His firm already let him work remotely two days a week, but was there really any reason he had to go into the office at all? His work was nearly entirely independent, and even without the bullying, the office was a distraction; he'd told her many times that he got twice as much done on his two days at home than in the three office days. Not to mention the commute time. Maybe the firm would consider shifting him to entirely remote? Or, failing that, only going into the office as needed—for all-hands meetings, face-to-faces with his boss, that sort of thing?

There was still urban living to take into account, though. And this house, however comfortable, was cheek-by-jowl with neighbors on all sides, traffic, noise, chaos, interruptions. Steph enjoyed city life, but David was never so relaxed and, well, himself, as when they were in their vacation home on Orcas Island.

Steph shut the fridge, sipped her wine, and thought.

Eventually she went back into the living room. "David?"

"Yes?" He looked up at her. The cocoa had restored some of his color, but he still looked so fragile.

"Let's move to Orcas full-time."

He stared at her. "What?"

"I know this is a big thing, and that you're not in a place to talk about it right now." She sat down beside him on the couch and took his hand. "But I think we should seriously consider it, and explore how we could make it happen."

"We can't!" It was the most animated he'd been since she'd gotten home. Which was…good? Maybe? "My job—they won't let me—"

"Again, you don't need this job. There are plenty of firms that would let you work a hundred percent remote." The more she thought about it, the better she liked the idea. But she couldn't push. They'd been through this pattern many times in their marriage: she got excited about something and wanted to rush ahead with it; he needed more time to adjust, to think it through, to… well, analyze it. He was an analyst, after all. She understood this, even respected it; she was at least as much of an outlier as he was, in the opposite direction. "But this is premature—we'd have a lot of things to figure out before we made any decisions." She smiled at him tentatively. "Promise me you'll think about it, at least? And we can talk about it this weekend maybe?"

He gave her a watery smile. He knew how this process went as well as she did, and he also knew—she was pretty sure that he knew—that if he still wasn't convinced after they had explored it, she would not steamroll him into anything. "Okay."

Last night

STEPH LAY IN bed beside David long after she'd switched off her bedside lamp. Was he asleep? He was quiet, and very still; he might be asleep, or he might wondering the same about her. Not wanting to say anything, and wake her up.

It had been so long since they'd shared a bed. They'd clearly both forgotten how.

She should be fast asleep by now. She was certainly tired enough. She'd worked hard all week, and extra-hard all day, preparing for the Christmas party; and then there had been the party itself, which had been exhausting and exhilarating as parties always were; and *then* there had been the unexpected situation at the end of the evening: a sudden snowstorm, a tree down on Deer Harbor Road, trapping their last ten guests here overnight. Or longer, depending on how quickly the county could get out to clear the road—of both the tree and the snow.

Lynne, next door, had been able to take two of the guests, but her house was tiny—hardly much expanded from the cabin she'd moved here into fifteen or more years ago, with her then-teenage son. That had left eight extra people to be squeezed into every possible corner of Steph and David's house…a large house, to be sure, but stretched to capacity now.

So that David had had to come back to the marital bed.

Steph rolled onto her side, facing him. He was curled up with his back to her, so she couldn't see if his eyes were open, and he didn't react to her movement. The room had that unreal glow that snow brought, especially under moonlight; had it stopped falling, then? She hoped so. She loved her friends, and she enjoyed having overnight guests, but such things were even better if they had actually been planned for. Everyone was going to want to get home, back to their lives, and pets, and responsibilities.

And Steph had been looking forward to the satisfaction of having the party, fun as it was, behind her.

The quiet was astonishing. Snow (even without the downed tree) had stopped what little traffic would normally be out at this hour, covered every sound the night woods usually made. It was both cozy and a little unsettling, to be awake, safe and warm inside, under a blanket of snow, under the hush of the world outside.

Before she'd turned off the light, she'd told David, "We have to talk." He'd agreed, of course; he was always agreeable. He was a good man. He loved her; he wanted their marriage to work as much as she did, if not more. Sometimes, in her less charitable moments, Steph wondered what in the world he would have done if he hadn't met her—if she hadn't ambushed him at the dim sum shop and basically demanded that they date; and then later, that they marry, build a life together. Would he have just stayed in his little rental room in the city, estranged from his awful parents, working for companies who didn't appreciate him but needed him? Depositing his paychecks into an ever-growing bank account, because he didn't want anything more than to be left alone to do his work, solve the puzzles that were so inscrutable to everyone else but were a delightful challenge to his powerful, unusual mind?

"You humanize me," he had joked, many times over the years. But he wasn't wrong. Steph brought life and friends and halfway decent furniture—and, of course, excellent food—into his world. She encouraged him out of his shell, as much as he was willing, or able.

"You ground me," she always told him in return, and that wasn't wrong either. Steph's passion, her fearlessness, her quest for adventure, could turn into impulsiveness and novelty-seeking for its own sake if not for David's counter-balancing effect. They made a really successful team, when things were working as they should.

Things had not been working as they should for some time

now.

Though he'd been reluctant, even terrified, at first, it had soon become clear that the move to Orcas Island had been the best decision they'd ever made—even better than their decision to marry, in her opinion. They had owned a small home here for years before that, loving to vacation amid the island's serene beauty. Thriving in the peace and quiet. Steph had always had a vague idea of maybe retiring someday to the island…but when David's mental health was challenged by his toxic workplace one time too many, she'd done some research, run the numbers, and presented him with her plan: sell the Sunnyvale house, put the proceeds into expanding and remodeling the Orcas house, and pull up stakes.

This plan hinged on David telling his firm that he needed to be a full-time remote employee or that he would leave altogether: their choice. Which sounded simple enough, and for someone whose early years had not been a minefield of shaming, belittling, and outright abuse on the part of his parents, it would have been. It had taken David nearly six months, and the very limit of Steph's gentle yet unceasing support and reassurance, but he had finally gone to his bosses and told them his demands.

Of course they had reacted as badly as he'd feared they would. They'd fussed and complained, declared that it was impossible for anyone to be remote full time, and even threatened him with legal action due to breach of contract. More than once—more than a dozen times—David was ready to give them what they wanted, but Steph always talked him out of it. And in the end, the firm had no leg to stand on, so they capitulated.

Steph had intended to find another job up on the island, once they got settled and she was finished overseeing the remodel, but it was true, what she had told him: they really didn't need her salary, and she relished not having to process forms in an insurance office all day. The remodel itself took several years, during which time she also put in a couple greenhouses and a marvelous vegetable garden, which of course needed tending. She dove even more deeply into the culinary arts, not just cooking and baking but also canning, pickling, and drying.

It was when she began looking into sausage-making, investing in a professional grade meat grinder and all the attachments that went with it, as well as reaching out to the various ranchers on the island for a supply of fresh meats, that she finally admitted to herself that she wasn't interested in looking for even a part-time job at the bakery or the bookstore. Her feminist nature bristled at labeling herself a housewife or a homemaker, but the truth of the matter was, Steph was happiest when she was cooking, planning meals, and tending to their comfortable home.

And sharing that home and all this bounty with her friends, of course. But was it enough? Sometimes—often—it felt like enough. Steph's days were full of engaging activity and interesting friends. David had seemed happy too. Or was he just coasting?

Were they both coasting?

Steph now sighed softly and rolled onto her back, staring at the ceiling. *This isn't right. There must be something wrong with me—I cannot figure out how to talk to my own damn husband.*

Should they have tried harder to adopt? After shying away from the idea of fertility treatments, they had looked into adoption, and had even registered with an agency, but it had all been so…daunting. So complicated. Not just the huge financial investment, for something they had not been one hundred percent convinced they'd wanted to begin with, but the emotional challenges as well—should it be an open adoption? Did they want to interview prospective birth mothers, who were of course assessing their suitability as well? Wasn't it enough just to be auntie and uncle to her sister Alexis's two boys?

Ultimately, they'd let their adoption agency registration lapse, had stopped returning their agency representative's phone calls, and essentially set the whole question down. And, a few years later, they had moved to Orcas Island.

It had been a classic frog-in-the-pot scenario, their quiet mutual distance. Turning toward other things more than turning away from each other. David had immediately thrived in full-time remote work, as she'd known he would, but trying to get his work done while living in an active construction site had been challenging, so they'd rented him office space in Eastsound. When the remodel was finally complete, David kept the office space, because he liked the occasional change of scenery, and also he'd moved a lot of equipment and furniture there, and didn't want to clutter up his clean new home study with it.

So he divided his time between the house and the town office, according to some inscrutable schedule of his own devising; Steph was never entirely sure where he would be on any given day. But at least he'd kept the reliable hours of the working West Coast brokerage employee: signing in at six a.m., a half-hour before Wall Street's opening bell; signing out at one in the afternoon.

It was when he'd gotten into day trading and exploring foreign markets that the frog's water had started to heat up. David had been so good at his regular job duties that he had of course gotten bored, so he'd explored other puzzles with which to challenge his mind. Steph had been happy for him—he excitedly tried to explain to her the systems he'd come up with for playing these new markets, and since he wasn't risking any of the capital they had built up for retirement (and he still had his well-paying job), she was delighted that he'd found this new endeavor. And he hadn't had any notable emotional crises in several years.

So she'd gone on with building her own life here on the island: joining a book group which morphed into a soup group; deepening her friendships with her next-door neighbor Lynne and the friends Lynne had introduced her to.

She'd drawn the line at playing pickleball, however. Lynne had tried any number of times to lure her in: "Just give it a try! It's fun!"

But Steph was having none of it. "I'm not sporty, and I'm not old enough anyway."

"Old enough! Teenagers play pickleball."

"I only see gray heads out there on the courts whenever I drive by. And besides, isn't it dangerous?"

"Dangerous?" Lynne had scoffed. "Not at all."

"Didn't you tell me about that woman who had to get airlifted off a few months ago? The one with the horribly broken ankle?"

"She tripped—could have happened to anyone, anywhere. That wasn't pickleball's fault."

"But she was trying to make a shot when it happened?"

Lynne had just laughed. "All right, your loss."

It did still feel weird to not work, all these years later, to keep letting David be the sole bread winner. When she'd mentioned this to some of her friends, they were very supportive and encouraging, of course. "Do what makes you happy," Lynne had told her, when they'd talked about this at Steph's soup group meeting last summer. "It seems to me that keeping this lovely home and garden, and taking care of David, is absolutely legitimate and valuable work—and you obviously enjoy it."

"You could open a restaurant," Alicia had said, and then, seeing the aghast look of horror on Steph's face, had laughed and amended her suggestion: "Or a catering business. Super exclusive, super high-end. Take three clients a year, or only work in the summer months, or whatever. Because food is your *thing*, and as you keep saying, at least half the joy is sharing it."

"I just don't know if I need to make a business of it," Steph had answered. "That's such a good way to ruin a perfectly fun hobby."

"I don't know about that," Julie had said. "My hobby is my business, and it just keeps getting more interesting and fulfilling all the time." Julie owned Paper Magic, a gift shop in town where she sold her own beautiful handmade books.

"Yeah, but you're, I don't know…" Steph had said. Julie smiled quizzically at her. "You're good at business, I guess."

"I had never run a business before I opened the shop," Julie said. "One doesn't know until one tries."

"I hadn't been in business for myself either, before I took on my first client," Alicia, a freelance children's book editor, pointed out. "And I'm sure you would be great at it. You're smart and organized and energetic and sensible."

Steph sighed softly again. *I don't* feel *smart and sensible.* She rolled onto her side, this time facing away from David. He still hadn't moved. Was she ever going to fall asleep? She didn't want to poke at her smartwatch and see what time it was. If she didn't know, she could pretend it wasn't that late...that she would get enough sleep if she just fell asleep soon...

And then it was morning, and the weird nighttime moon-on-snow light had become jarringly bright sun-on-snow light, pouring through the clerestory windows above her bed. She heard movement out in the house—somebody clearly trying to be quiet.

Time to get up, then. She had a house full of guests!

Steph sat up, blinked the sleep out of her eyes, and was up and into her robe and halfway to her bathroom before she thought to look back at the bed. David! She had been sleeping alone for so long, she'd almost forgotten him.

Was he still asleep?

No: the bed was empty.

Was he already out making coffee for the guests? Or had he gone to hide somewhere? He wasn't going to be able to get into his study if Julie and her boyfriend Gavin were still in there, and nobody on this whole side of the island was likely to have driven anywhere yet.

Steph quickly went through her morning ablutions, pulled on some jeans and a warm sweatshirt, and went out to see what was what.

Soft voices came from the kitchen; in the other direction, both guest room doors and the study door were closed. Steph padded out to the kitchen and found David, along with Julie's grown daughters, Megan and Lori, sitting around the breakfast table, mugs of coffee before each of them, and a platter of sliced banana bread between them.

Wow.

Steph smiled and headed for the coffee pot. "Good morning, everyone," she said.

Megan looked up at her. "Hey—David got us some sustenance."

David gave Steph a shy smile. "I hope that was okay."

"Okay? That was perfect!" Steph poured herself a mug of coffee, doctored it, and brought it to the table. "Was this in the kitchen freezer?" she asked him, taking a piece of banana bread. He'd even warmed it.

"Yeah. I didn't see a label, but I saved the plastic and foil, if you want to double check."

"Thank you." She took a bite. "That was just the right thing to do."

He looked relieved, though she'd explained the system to him plenty of times: the house fridge, and its freezer, were stocked with food that was available for eating—unless it was labeled otherwise. The garage fridge and its freezer were for overflow and backup items—mostly prepared (by Steph, of course) foods, ready for thawing on days when she didn't feel like making something new or ran out of time to cook. These were kept track of in a spreadsheet, so she'd know when she needed to replenish them. The chest freezer in the garage was mostly for raw material and ingredients—ground beef and lamb and pork from Lum Farm, salmon filets from Troller Point, fresh homemade pasta, summer fruits and berries—and were also in the spreadsheet.

"This is delicious," Lori said, picking up a slice of banana bread—clearly not her first, judging by the crumbs on her plate.

"Thanks." Steph smiled as she took a bite of her own. "It's most just the old Joy of Cooking recipe, but I made a few tweaks."

"Do I smell coffee?" came a voice from the doorway. It was their friend Matt, looking cute and rumpled.

"You certainly do," Steph said, leaping up. "Come on in—there's one cup left in this pot, so take it and I'll brew another."

On her way to the coffee machine, she turned back and caught a glimpse of Matt and Megan sharing a glance…yep, just as she'd thought last night. There was a spark there.

Too bad he lived here on Orcas while Megan lived down in Portland, Oregon. Well, geography wasn't destiny, was it?

With a secret smile, Steph turned back to the counter and got him a mug.

Chapter 2

RON

It made Ron uncomfortable to be a passenger in a car. Pretty much when anyone but him was driving; but especially when it was Alicia.

Yet even Ron had to admit that Alicia was the far better driver on snow and ice. So he gritted his teeth and forced himself to sit still and quiet while she navigated their way home, late on Sunday afternoon, when the county finally got the roads cleared and passable.

"Relax," Alicia said, after making the turn onto Orcas Road from Deer Harbor.

"I'm fine," he ground out, clutching tightly at his door handle.

"We could have stayed another night," she said, obviously answering his tone and body language, not his words. "Steph clearly would have enjoyed it—even David didn't look like he was hating it all that much."

"I said I'm *fine*." He stared straight ahead at the slushy road. The county called this *cleared*? Could have fooled him.

"I'm not sure I've ever exchanged so many words with David, the whole time I've known them," Alicia went on, as if she hadn't heard Ron. Of all the things she did that annoyed him, this was…well, certainly one of them. Nobody liked to feel not-listened-to, and this was basically a blatant announcement: *"I'm not hearing you! You might as well not be here!"* Fine, he would just stop talking then.

A moment later, though, he couldn't stand it. "We agreed we need to get home," he bit out. Okay, *now* he was done talking.

She shrugged, and took the corner by Nordstroms Lane far too fast, in his opinion. Somehow the car held onto the road. "I mean, I'll be happy to get home too, sure, and get into different clothes, sleep in our own bed. But it was kinda fun, getting trapped there. Like a big slumber party."

Ron just turned and glared at her. If she noticed, she didn't let on.

"Matt's dad was definitely confused this morning, though," Alicia went on. "I feel for him."

"For who?" Ron said, unable to help himself. "The old man, or Matt?"

"Well, both of them, I guess. Matt works so hard to take care of him; I wonder if his dad even realizes it. How much Matt is giving up to do this."

"You mean his girlfriend leaving him? She was never right for him." She'd fled when the old man's dementia had become more challenging, though she'd pretended that wasn't the reason.

"Not just Heather." It was nearly dark out, despite not even being four o'clock yet; Alicia was still driving too fast, though she seemed entirely relaxed and in command of the wheel. Well, she probably thought she was. "But certainly that's part of it—and you're wrong, by the way. She was a sweetheart."

"If she were such a *sweetheart*, she wouldn't have left him when things got tough."

Alicia exhaled through her nose. Was she mocking him? She'd been doing this more and more lately. "Nobody can know what goes on inside someone else's relationship. Heck, I think even the people *in* the relationship can't really know everything."

Good lord, she hits on something cogent just when I least expect it, Ron thought snarkily, but wisely kept his mouth shut. *Don't annoy the woman who holds your life in her hands.*

Though Ron wasn't entirely sure if he *could* annoy Alicia anymore. She just chirpily skipped through life, bubbling with enthusiasm, oblivious to his moods, his needs, his opinions. *Not listening* to him.

She hadn't always been this way, of course. She'd hung on his every word when they'd first met, when he'd been the older, sophisticated English professor and she'd been the starry-eyed young editor. An editor of *juvenile* literature at that. He'd thought she was perfect: intellectual, or at least not stupid; but sufficiently in awe of his greater intelligence and breadth of knowledge.

She'd been sexy too—a hot little number. Sure, she was still attractive—it was good that she kept herself in shape—but now that she was in her fifties, that naif gamine act was wearing a little thin.

For some insane reason, Alicia signaled and then turned in at Main Street, to cut across town rather than going around on Lover's Lane and Mt. Baker Road. WHY? Ron bit his lip; it was too late, the deed was done.

Just another example of how she never listened to him. The speed limit on Mt. Baker—once you passed the health clinic—was 35, whereas in town it was 20. Okay, fine, she probably shouldn't be going 35 with the roads in the condition they were right now, but still. He'd explained this to her time and time again, that it was always faster to go around, not risk getting stuck behind a line of tourists in town, fresh off the ferry.

This way they'd have to go along Crescent Beach, as well—a road that was flooded half the time in winter. God only knew what it would look like today. Probably black ice.

He gripped his door handle harder and closed his eyes. If they made it home alive, he would never get into a car with her again.

Why couldn't Alicia be gentle and kind with him, like Steph was to her weirdo freak of a husband? You never saw the guy, but then there he was this morning, pretending to act like a halfway normal person—and there Steph was, looking at him with affection. With love.

Ron would give anything to see that look...

No. Stop, he told himself. It wasn't going to happen, and he didn't *want* it to happen, and that was just that. The grass is always greener, and blah blah blah. Probably Steph would grate on his nerves after he got to know her as well as he knew Alicia.

Almost certainly.

Everyone did, in the end.

He had learned this lesson the first time with Gena. There should be a law against marrying your college sweetheart! Nobody's mind was even halfway formed in college, no matter how much information you stuffed in there. The age of consent for marriage ought to be thirty, at a very minimum. Romance—sex—affairs at any age, sure; but no shackling yourself legally to someone until you were sufficiently mature.

And *certainly* no reproducing.

Ron wasn't sorry he'd had children. Of course not. He just wished both he and Gena had been a little older when they'd had Cynthia...okay, a *lot* older. They were really just kids themselves—Gena was pregnant before they'd even finished undergrad. They weren't ready, not even a little bit. And then, being so young and naïve, they'd gone on and compounded the error by following Cyn with Scott and then Ben, bing-bang-boom, all while Ron was still laboring through his Ph.D. program. Trying to concentrate in a tiny house with three kids under five—two of them still in diapers.

Still. It wasn't fair of Gena to claim that Ron had been a grouchy, stern, hands-off father. What was he supposed to do? *Not* get his doctorate, *not* get a decent university job that kept a roof over their heads and food on their table?

He sighed and shook away the memory of the stale old argument, and saw that he'd missed noticing the condition of the road by Crescent Beach; Alicia was slowing down for the stop sign at Olga Road. God, nearly the home stretch already. They might make it there alive after all.

He was exhausted by the time Alicia pulled into their driveway, set the brake, and turned off the car. "There! That wasn't so bad." She gave him an innocent smile. "Let's get in there and get that house warmed up, hm? And then we can figure out what to do for dinner."

Did she seriously imagine that he'd be able to eat a bite, after a ride like that? He was permanently emotionally scarred. He stifled a shudder. "I'll open a bottle of wine."

JULIE

JULIE PAGED THROUGH her recipe binder, looking for inspiration. The next soup group meeting, in just over a week, was her turn to host. She'd done Rancho Gordo's midnight black bean soup last time, which had been hearty and a little spicy—quite delicious. She still wanted something hearty and warm for winter, but she hated to repeat herself, or even do something too close to what she'd done before.

Clam chowder? Beef stew? So unimaginative.

Chicken and dumplings? Not technically a soup, but if she made it extra brothy...

Gavin sat on the other end of her sofa, reading a book. He seemed engrossed. Megan and Lori, who had arrived before Christmas, were leaving tomorrow; they were at the grocery store right now, shopping for their final dinner here, which they insisted they wanted to cook for Julie and Gavin. "You've been so sweet to let us stay here for so long!" Megan had said. "We want to give back."

"You've been so sweet to come all this way to spend a week and a half with your dear old mother," Julie had countered. "On her boring old island out past the edge of nowhere."

Megan had given her a joyful smile. "Oh, it's not the least bit boring around here."

Julie was pretty sure Megan and Matt had had lunch or coffee at least twice…but nobody was telling her anything, so she kept her mouth shut. If Megan (or Matt, for that matter) wanted to know what Julie thought, they could ask. Otherwise, she'd stay out of it.

But oooh, she had thoughts. And feelings.

On the face of it, Megan-and-Matt as a couple was a great idea. Matt was a sweetheart; Julie had always been very fond of him. He was also stable and responsible—as evidenced by the fact that he'd taken his father in—and made a good living with his web design business. He owned his own home. He cared about the community, obviously. He cooked good soup.

But as for the intangible, irrational side of things…he couldn't date her *daughter*! Matt was Julie's *friend*! It made zero sense, she knew, but friends went in one category and daughters went into another category, and those elements just should not mix.

He's not that much older than she is, Julie told herself, now staring unseeingly at the recipe binder. Not even ten years. *But, it's just…just wrong!*

"What's the matter?" Gavin asked, looking up from his book. "What?"

He smiled gently at her. "You keep sighing. Is the soup group really that hard? Maybe I don't want to join after all."

"I was sighing?" She set the binder down. "I guess I was. I was thinking about Megan and Matt."

Gavin cocked his head. "I think they like each other."

"I think so too."

"Is that a problem?"

She stifled another sigh. "No? I don't think so. I just, it's weird, is all."

Gavin set his book on the coffee table. It was a collection of short stories that Julie had bought years ago, as inspiration for her pithies, though she hadn't ended up using it for that. "Your daughters have had relationships before, right?"

"Oh, sure! They're both in their thirties—Megan started dating in high school. Lori was a little more slow to get boy-crazy, but she more than made up for lost time in college." Julie smiled at the memory.

"So it's just that now she's interested in a friend of yours?"

"That's dumb, isn't it?" Julie gave him a helpless smile. "It's like—too many changes too fast, or something. I still haven't gotten used to it not being Matt-and-Heather, though she left him months ago."

"Do you think it's too soon for him?" Gavin asked. "That he's on a rebound?"

"Maybe," Julie admitted. "He's a fantastic man, but yeah, he might not be good relationship material right now. But Megan is smart. She won't jump into anything that isn't a good idea for her."

"Also she lives in Portland, and she has a job and an apartment and a life there and everything," Gavin pointed out. "Even if they do start something, it'll likely be long distance, at least for a while. That'll slow things up."

"Good point." She shrugged. "And it's really no business of mine, when it comes down to it. They're both adults."

"I think as her mother, you have every right to have opinions about it."

Julie leaned over and gave him a quick kiss. "Have I told you today how wonderful you are?"

Gavin pulled her closer and kissed her, less quickly and more thoroughly. "I'm not sure if you have. Tell me again."

She laughed, and felt her whole body flush with desire. "Well then—"

The door rattled, and in walked Megan and Lori. "Here we are! Home from the store!" Megan sang out, comically loud. "Sure hope we're not *interrupting* anything!"

Julie laughed and scooted back off of Gavin's lap, straightening her blouse. "Not at all! We were just talking about how excited we are—"

Lori snorted.

"—that you girls are going to cook such a nice dinner for us!" Julie finished, giving her daughters an innocent smile.

"Hope you like mushrooms, Gavin," Megan said, heading into the kitchen with a full shopping bag. "They had an assortment of fresh wild mushrooms, and I couldn't resist them."

"Mushrooms!" Julie exclaimed, grabbing her recipe binder again. One problem solved, at least! "A mushroom soup—creamy and hearty—that's perfect for winter. Let me see…"

STEPH

OF COURSE DAVID would have fallen easily back into their routine, if she'd let him.

So she didn't let him.

"It feels weird to me to share this house, this life, with you and live entirely separately," she'd told him, after all their stranded guests had gone home and the Christmas party had been cleaned up. "I'd like you to stay sleeping in our bed, if that's all right with you."

David had widened his eyes, but he had agreed.

After a few days had gone by and the world hadn't ended, Steph broached another topic as she was preparing dinner. David had stopped in the kitchen for a snack; she corralled him on his way to the fridge.

"Hey, actually, I have a question. I would like to start having our dinners together again—at least four or five times a week, if not every day."

David paused in the middle of the kitchen and stared at her. "Do I have to come to your soup group?"

Steph shrugged. "You don't *have* to do anything you don't want to do," she said gently. "But the folks in the group are really nice. You could give it a try? You seemed to like them when they all stayed overnight here after the party."

"They're not all nice," David muttered, looking at his feet.

"Except for Ron, they're all super nice," Steph said. "And he's just...kind of a curmudgeon."

"It's more than that," David said. "He makes me uncomfortable."

"Well, then don't come to soup groups," she said, trying not to sound exasperated. Because she knew what he meant, and he wasn't wrong. Ron was an acquired taste...well, okay, Ron was kind of a bully. And David was of course particularly sensitive to bullies.

"He likes you," David blurted out.

Steph set the knife on the chopping block and turned fully to David, who had taken a seat at the kitchen table. "All of us in the group like each other," she said.

"You know what I mean." His blue eyes met hers. "He likes you, and he doesn't think much of me."

"Oh David." Steph walked over and sat beside him, leaning her head on his strong shoulder. She stifled the urge to say something minimizing like *He would like you if you got to know him*. It wasn't true; and Steph believed in telling the truth. Particularly to her husband, the man she'd chosen to share her life with.

He put his arm around her and hugged her to his side, awkward in the wooden chairs, but doable. They sat like that for a minute, communicating without talking. Eventually, she said, "So, what about just making sure you and I have dinner together most evenings? Can you do that? Starting tonight, maybe? I'm roasting a chicken."

He pulled her tighter to him, then kissed the top of her head. "Okay."

She smiled at him. "Thanks."

After a moment where he just held her, he drew back and said,

"Steph, what are you even doing with me?"

She pulled back as well and looked at him. "What do you mean?"

He sighed. "What kind of wife has to beg her husband to have dinner with her? What's the matter with me? You don't deserve this."

"Don't start that," she said, softly. "What's going on with you right now? Have you been taking your meds?"

"Yes, always," he said, a little vehemently.

She knew he didn't lie to her either. So that was a relief, at least. "What about exercising? When was the last time you went to the gym?"

He looked sheepish. "Um. Maybe a few weeks ago?" At her look, he went on. "It's hard in the winter."

"I know. But you know what a difference it makes with your depression—"

"I know, I do," he said. "I'm sorry. I'm just lazy…"

She shook her head. "No, cut that out too. When you start beating yourself up, you just spiral down faster." She reached up and touched his cheek. "Action plans, and looking forward: remember? Do you want my help refocusing? Setting a schedule for the gym?"

"No, I can do it."

She held his gaze, and then nodded. "I believe you. And I do still want to keep sleeping in the same bed, and also having dinner together—oh, let's say five nights a week. Monday through Friday. Does that work?"

"Yes."

"You can even tell me what time you'd like to eat."

He looked like he wanted to protest again, but he didn't. "I could do seven," he said instead. "That leaves me four hours to do whatever the overseas markets need after my regular workday, and time enough to get home if I'm in town."

The overseas markets don't need anything from you, Steph thought, but she just smiled. "Great. Let's try that—for two weeks. And we'll check back in at the end of the two weeks and talk about what worked and what didn't, okay?"

He nodded again, looking sheepish. "I still don't think I deserve you."

She rolled her eyes. "I don't care what story you need to tell yourself about it. I just want to see you across the dinner table."

"You will."

LYNNE

OH MY GOODNESS gracious, Lynne thought, standing before the closet in her guest room—Ethan's room. The craft room. Whatever. The closet was piled high with fabrics and notions, as well as completed works. *Where do I even begin?*

Steph's friend Kate, who ran a gallery in town, had stayed here with her husband on the night everyone was stranded. And she had offered to exhibit Lynne's work—*in a one-woman show!* In *May!* Which would be here before she knew it—it was already nearly the middle of January, and Lynne had no idea what she was going to put in the show. Should she make new works for it? She'd have to. None of this stuff was good enough to display in public.

She exhaled a big breath and closed the closet, then went and sat on the guest bed/Ethan's bed. *I'm too old for this*, she thought. *I'm a semi-retired doctor. I'm not an artist. I just do this for fun. To keep my hands busy. Kate was just being polite. She didn't really mean it...*

Lynne didn't even believe herself, though. She knew she was talented, that she had an eye for color and design, and that her hands were skilled and precise. She had been graciously accepting compliments for her craft work for decades.

But this was just...a whole new level of exposure. It felt fraught.

"Why?" she asked herself aloud, getting up and going into the kitchen. She poured herself a glass of white wine and sipped it. "What am I risking, anyway? This should just be a fun thing. Right?"

She took the wine to the living room and sank into her plush chair, then suddenly laughed at herself. "And here's the dotty old lady doctor, talking to an empty house. As if the walls are going to answer. Why don't you try talking to a real person?" Not Steph, though; Kate was Steph's friend, and Steph was naturally fearless and wouldn't be any help anyway. Lynne needed someone else's opinion...someone who already was comfortable showing her artistic creations to the world, and unafraid to ask people to spend good money on them.

She picked up the phone next to her and dialed Julie.

"Hey," Julie said, sounding pleased but a little surprised. "What's up?"

"I want to run something by you." She could hear voices in the background. "Oh, you're busy, sorry."

"I am—but I can talk for a bit. Or, hang on a second, I have a better idea." She must have covered the phone with her hand to talk to someone; Lynne heard muffled voices, both Julie's and those of several other people. Then she returned to the line. "Come for dinner. It'll be ready in half an hour—you just have time to get here."

"What? I don't need..."

"My daughters are making the biggest mushroom feast you've ever seen," Julie interrupted her. "It's their last night here, and they're making pasta, and pizzas, *and* tarts. There's enough food here for ten people, and it won't be nearly as good left over as it is tonight. You come and help us eat it, and we can talk about whatever you like. Okay?"

Lynne only thought about it for a moment. "That sounds nice, but are you sure? You want to share your girls on their last night?"

Julie laughed. "They'll be back."

She sounded quite certain of herself. "All right," Lynne said.

"I'll come. What can I bring?"

"Nothing, seriously—you should see this kitchen. There isn't room for another ramekin."

Nevertheless, Lynne grabbed an unopened bottle of Pinot Grigio on her way out the door.

She parked by the dug-up concrete in front of Julie's store, still here from the aborted parking meter snafu from last fall. What a dumb idea that had been! Lynne wondered when, or if, the county was going to repair the sidewalk. Perhaps never—maybe it would just become one of those things, part of the landscape which everybody ultimately stopped seeing.

It was a festive atmosphere in Julie's little house. Both of her daughters and Gavin seemed to fill up the place, almost as much as the soup group meetings did. Julie took the wine bottle that Lynne handed her and carried it off to the kitchen, where Lori opened it and splashed a little into her own glass before handing it to her sister.

"Let's leave them to it," Julie said, laughing and handing Lynne a glass of wine. "They swear they're almost done, but I bet we have time to talk for a few minutes." She steered Lynne back into the living room; Gavin followed. "Or did you want privacy for this?" Julie asked, glancing at her boyfriend.

"No, not at all." Then she laughed. "I mean, I don't think so; but I'm feeling so unsettled, I'm not even sure what I want."

"I can make myself scarce," Gavin said, starting to leap up from the couch where he'd just sat.

"No, don't!" Lynne hurried to say. "I'd actually welcome your point of view as well."

"All right," Julie said, as they got settled. "What's up?"

Lynne took a breath. "How did you know you wanted to put your own creative products out in the world—when was the first time you really felt comfortable doing that?"

Julie gave a surprised laugh. "Huh, wow. So you think I feel comfortable doing that?" She turned to Gavin. "I sure have her fooled!"

"But you don't," Lynne said, more seriously. Gavin nodded agreement. "You work full-time creating and sharing your books. I've known you for years, Julie Pessel; you didn't take this on lightly, and you wouldn't have even considered it if it hadn't been what you really, really wanted to do."

Julie sipped her wine and sat back, still smiling. "All right, you win: I didn't just stumble into this behind my own back. I decided I wanted to make a go of it, and I worked hard." She leaned forward and held Lynne's gaze. "But the reason I did it? It was because I couldn't stand the idea of doing anything else. I pretty much felt that it was my only option, you know?"

"I think I do know, but tell me more."

"It was not long after I decided to move here. I had a supposedly good job in San Francisco, but I hated it. My girls both lived in Portland; I wanted to be closer to them—"

"But not *too* close!" Megan sang out from the kitchen.

Julie chuckled. "True, this is a little farther than I'd hoped, but at least it's not twelve hours of I-5 away. Anyway: I knew I didn't want to find another job working for someone else, and that I wanted to do something creative. And I wanted to live here—but that's all I knew, really. I didn't know what any of this would look like, when it came right down to it." She glanced at Gavin, who gave her an encouraging smile back. "I actually thought I'd write novels," Julie went on, "but then when I came to look at property on the island, I found this place, and immediately knew I was home. The decision sort of made itself at that point."

"A house behind and a shop in front," Lynne said. "But how did you know what you wanted that shop to be? You could have opened a café, or a bookstore, or even something real estate-related, like what you used to do."

Julie shrugged. "I don't really know how to explain it. It was just, when I saw the shop, I just *knew* what should be on those shelves. I could almost see them there already." She tilted her head. "So, are you going to tell me why you're full of all these questions? Are you thinking about opening a store to sell your pieces?"

"Ha!" Lynne exclaimed. "No, not that...but Kate Evintrude has invited me to have a solo show at her gallery in May."

Julie squealed with excitement, bringing both girls rushing out of the kitchen to find out why. "That's so amazing!" Megan said, when she heard. "We will come for opening night!"

"Of course we will!" Lori said, nearly hopping up and down with excitement.

Gavin beamed at Lynne. "You wanted my input too? I say, congratulations and go for it! What even is the question here?"

Lynne laughed. "Okay, well, we seem to have a quorum..."

"Oh, and by the way," Lori said, "dinner's ready. Are we squeezing everyone around the table, or eating on our laps out here?"

"Laps," Julie said, and hopped up. "It's what we do for soup group. Come on, everyone, let's get it while it's hot!"

It was a few minutes before everyone was settled back in the living room with plates piled high with fungus-inflected delicacies. Lynne munched a shiitake-gruyère tart and wiped crumbs from the corner of her mouth. "This is amazing," she told the girls. "I want this recipe."

"Of course," Megan said with a smile. "I'll text it to you."

They ate and chatted about the meal and mushrooms in general for a few minutes, but soon, Julie leaned over to Lynne and asked in a lower voice, "So, you're feeling uncertain about the solo show?"

Lynne sighed. "I am. And I can't really explain why. I just...I've been doing fiber arts of one kind or another all my life, but never with any recognition or commercial reward in mind. It was always for *me*, or for my family and loved ones. Being a doctor: that was my career. Those parts of me always felt important to keep separate, but I'm questioning why." She gave Julie a helpless smile. "So that's why I wanted to talk to you about it. You made the transition from a job that was just a job to doing something creative for a living. Not that I see making a living with my arts, or even needing to—but I can't even get over the little voice inside my head that says, *Who do you think you are? You're not an artist!*"

"We all have that voice, to one degree or another," Julie said. "I'm not going to just glibly tell you to ignore it, but—well, maybe I am, a bit. Let it say what it wants to say, and then go ahead and do what feeds your soul anyway."

"What feeds my soul right now is this pasta," Lynne said, feeling a little self-conscious about having brought her insecurities to Julie.

Julie laughed. "I'm going to miss these girls, and not just because of this yummy meal." She gazed fondly over at her daughters, who were sitting on either side of Gavin and tag-teaming telling him a story. What would it have been like to have more than one kid, Lynne wondered. Ethan always maintained that he was happy being an only child, but Megan and Lori seemed like best friends as well as siblings.

It sure hadn't been that way with Lynne's siblings, growing up. And now her older sister was in a nursing home back east, while her younger brother was still in southern California...she thought. It had been years since they'd exchanged so much as a Christmas card.

Then she shook her head, bringing herself back to the moment. Boy, she really didn't want to face these anxieties, did she? All the more reason to do so, then. "Julie, thank you. This has been really helpful."

Julie shrugged and took a bite of pasta. "I'm not sure for what—I don't think I told you anything you don't already know."

Lynne smiled at her. "Maybe, maybe not. I think it's what you're showing me even more than telling me."

"Oh?"

Lynne gestured around the small room. "Look at this—a cozy,

welcoming space, filled with your own works and things you love. And with people you love." They both looked at Gavin, Megan, and Lori, now laughing heartily. "I have been very happy in my little house out in Deer Harbor, but it's...rather quieter than this, I'm now realizing. I think I've been perching there, hiding there, instead of living there." She took a breath and squared her shoulders. "And now, metaphorically anyway, Kate Evintrude has invited me to town—and it scared me to pieces. I'm terrified of the exposure, but also so, so excited for it."

"That's wonderful!" Julie exclaimed. "The excitement part, I mean."

"Yeah." Lynne nodded. "Mostly."

"What are you going to put into the show, do you know?"

"Gah! That's the other thing. I have no idea! I was looking at my inventory and I clearly have to throw it all away and create an entirely new body of work."

Julie laughed aloud. "Perfect! You're right on schedule—I do that every time I'm about to bring out a new line, or even a tweak on an old line." She gave Lynne an encouraging grin. "Tell you what: if you're still feeling this way in a week, I'll come over and take a look at your inventory. We can figure it out together."

"You're the best." They exchanged warm smiles, as Lynne wondered if she would ever feel this confident. "I will take you up on that."

Chapter 3

STEPH

After a week, things had been going so well, Steph decided to celebrate. Besides, Friday night was traditionally date night, wasn't it?

So she set about making all of David's favorite foods—well, all his favorite Asian foods, anyway; if she'd made *all* his favorites, it would have been a meal for twenty.

She was rolling up the spicy orange-scented Chinese meatballs when he came into the kitchen, smiling at her. "Smells amazing in here—ooh, are those what I think they are?"

"They are," she said, leaning back for his quick kiss. "But what you're smelling is the soup."

He gave a pretend frown. "I thought you told me I didn't have to go to your soup group meetings."

"There's no rule that says we can only eat soup once every two weeks," she said with a laugh.

He sniffed, and then leaned over the stove, lifting the lid on the soup pot. "Especially if the soup in question is ginger-lemongrass. Is all this just for me?"

"Well, I was sort of hoping to have some too."

David laughed. "I will be happy to share with you. Seven o'clock?"

"Yep." He was on his way back out the kitchen door when she added, "And it's a date night, by the way, so put on something nice. If you like."

"Sure thing. I'll meet you at the table at seven—if you don't need any help here."

"No, I'm good, but thanks."

He headed down the hall, Steph smiling at his back.

An hour later, she was extra glad she'd decided to change for dinner, because the meatballs splattered and spat all over her as she was sautéing them. The ginger-orange sauce was too liquidy, or the pan was too hot; Steph wasn't sure. The end result was delicious—she'd snuck one just to be sure—but the kitchen was a disaster, as were her jeans and sweatshirt.

Steph quickly washed her face and arms in their bathroom before changing into a little black cocktail dress. David had already come and gone; he had somewhat comically snuck past her on his way into the dining room a few minutes ago, so she'd averted her eyes so as not to see what he was up to.

She zipped up the back of the dress, thanking her past self for having the presence of mind to buy clothes with some stretch to them; then she checked her reflection one more time in the bathroom mirror before heading back to the kitchen. The soup was still hot on the back of the stove; the meatballs were keeping warm under the heat lamp; the salads with thinly sliced radishes, mandarin orange wedges and poppy seed dressing were keeping cool in the fridge.

Then she peered into the dining room. David was leaning over the table, rearranging flowers in the crystal vase her uncle had given them as a wedding present. Steph bit her lower lip, looking at David. His blond hair was neatly combed, and his blue eyes picked up the sparkles from the chandelier—and the candles he'd lit. He was wearing a dark suit and a pale blue shirt, and he looked *really* good.

"Oh my," she breathed. "Is that the suit I think it is?"

David looked up at her and smiled, patting his flat stomach. "Despite your cooking, I still fit into it."

"You goofball." She stepped into the room and pulled him into her arms. He smelled nice too—freshly bathed and shaved, and the suit looked crisp and didn't smell like mothballs either. Had he planned ahead? He couldn't have gotten the suit cleaned and pressed in an hour, when she asked him to dress up. "You look amazing—if I'd have known you were wearing your wedding outfit, I wouldn't have worn this."

He drew back and looked her up and down approvingly. "You look spectacular. Anyway, somehow I don't think of a white satin gown when I think of date night—with sticky meatballs."

She laughed, and leaned over the flower arrangement, sniffing at a rose. "These are gorgeous. Where did you find such nice flowers in January?"

He gave a mysterious smile. "I will never tell."

She rolled her eyes. "Still a goofball, but a sweet one. Anyway, I'll bring dinner in."

In the kitchen, she quickly assembled two plates with meatballs over jasmine rice, then ladled soup into matching bowls, sprinkling a tiny pinch of chives over each one. She brought the plates to the table, returning for the soup and salads. Meanwhile, David poured champagne into tall flutes.

They sat across from each other, grinning like teenagers on their first date. At last, Steph raised her glass; David lifted his and clinked it to hers lightly. "To us," she said softly.

"To us," he echoed, "and to you. Thank you for sticking with me."

"Of course," she said, her heart melting. "There was never a question. Thank you for being willing to show back up." She winced at her awkward grammar, but David only kept smiling at her.

"I never want to let you down, Steph," he said. "But I do sometimes need a reminder."

"Then I will remind you." She smiled and took a sip of her champagne. "Eat, my love, before everything gets cold."

He grinned back at her and dug in.

As they ate, she found herself telling him about the cookbook idea that had come up at soup group last fall. Not about Ron's ham-fisted attempt to take it over; she felt a little reluctant to discuss Ron with David, given his discomfort with the man. "I think it could be a fun project," she said. "And easy to put together the contents—it's pretty much already in place, with our database. We just have to choose which recipes to put in."

"That does sound like a fun idea," he agreed. "But it's going to be weirdly uneven, don't you think?"

"Uneven? What do you mean?"

He shrugged. "Well, your food is head and shoulders better than anyone else's. If everyone puts in an equal number of recipes, one-fifth of them are going to really stand out."

"Oh, that's not true," she said, scraping her bowl. "Everyone in the group does a good job."

"Didn't you tell me about a macaroni soup? With storebought meatballs?"

Steph laughed. "Matt only does that because his dad loves it. We won't put that one in the book."

"Are you at least going to help everyone with their recipes?" he asked. "So that they're not embarrassed?"

"You are too loyal, my love," she told him.

After dinner, he said, "I turned on the fire in the living room before we ate, if you want to finish our champagne in there."

Steph felt another wave of warm delight flow through her. "I would love that." She added with a smile, "I'll bring the dessert in there as well."

They left the dishes on the table and snuggled up on the sofa before the flickering flames. David tucked his arm around her and held her close; she luxuriated in the nearness of him, his warmth, his strength. She hadn't realized how much she'd missed this physical closeness.

They'd been sharing a bed for several weeks now, but so far they hadn't resumed more intimacy than occasional cuddling. Tonight, however...

She had barely begun the thought when David set his champagne flute down on the coffee table next to their empty ramekins, then leaned down and gave her a gentle kiss.

Steph kissed him back, savoring the flavors of champagne and sweet red-bean mousse on his lips, along with the barest hint of lemongrass which underlay the dessert flavors. Best of all was the unique, delicious taste that was David himself.

He sighed softly and pulled her closer, deepening their kiss. His hands began to caress her—her shoulders, her back, and lower.

Steph gave a small growl in the back of her throat and allowed her hands to explore him, nudging the suit jacket off his strong shoulders.

David kissed down her neck, nipping softly at her earlobe— something that drove her crazy, and that he hadn't done in years. She moaned and pressed against him, her hands still roaming.

After a few heated minutes, he pulled back and murmured, "Shall we move to our bed?"

"I'm comfortable here," she said, reaching for his belt buckle.

AFTERWARD, THEY LAY on the couch in each other's arms. Steph was practically purring with satisfaction. The flames of the gas fire made dancing patterns on the ceiling; David lazily played with a strand of her hair.

"Why did we ever stop doing that?" she mused aloud.

"Was that a rhetorical question, or did you want me to answer it?" he murmured.

She chuckled. "Rhetorical, I suppose; though if you ever want to talk about—well, anything—I am happy to."

He softly kissed her temple. "You know my issues. I don't have anything new to say about them, I don't think."

His issues... Steph felt a pang of sorrow amid her bliss. His depression and its close relative anxiety dated back to his very unhappy childhood. He did not often like to talk about his parents, who had been forceful, controlling presences in his life, deeply disappointed in their only child and not afraid to let him know about it. Steph had never met either of them; David had kicked them out of his life before she'd met him. It wasn't really any wonder that he was so introverted, preferring solitude, or that he was a natural target for bullies.

What was amazing was that he'd been willing to enter into a romantic partnership at all, and even to consider having children. Steph still sometimes wondered what she and David would have been like as parents, but she also often felt guiltily grateful that it hadn't worked out for them. No child would want to see their father huddled under a blanket on the couch, unable to cope with abusive coworkers...

"Yes," she whispered after a minute. "I do know your issues. But I'm glad they're not ruling your life these days."

"They don't seem to be." He caressed her shoulder absently. "I think this was just an inertia problem."

"Well, I'm glad we got things rolling again," she said sleepily.

The light of the flames flickered on the ceiling, easing her into a gentle dream.

ALICIA

SHE MISSED PICKLEBALL.

Play always slowed way down in the winter—nobody really enjoyed playing in the high school gym, especially given the limited hours that the space was available—but this winter had seemed worse than most. If it wasn't raining, it was literally freezing, with a dangerous skin of ice all over the courts; and if it stopped raining or freezing for five minutes, the winds howled, making batting a whiffleball around laughably impossible.

So no one had been out on the courts for weeks. There had been a brief moment of sunny forty-degree weather in the third week in January, but it had vanished almost as quickly as it had arrived, and now it was horribly wintry outside again.

She stirred the Welsh rarebit soup, hoping once again that the group wouldn't turn their noses up at her concoction. Well, of course they wouldn't—it wasn't a *gourmet* group, except for Steph—but she still felt a little self-conscious about making cheese-and-beer soup to ladle over a bed of toast, even for her group of very good friends.

Or maybe she was feeling self-conscious because Ron was being such a poop about it. He'd been surlier than usual these last few weeks—well, since before the new year, if she were honest. He was never much of a Mr. Sunshine, but lately…he didn't ever have a nice thing to say about anything, or anyone.

Especially about Alicia, or anything that she was doing.

Did I choose a (literally) cheesy dinner on purpose to rankle him? she asked herself now. She didn't think so—she'd been wanting to make this one from the first time she'd run across the recipe, and it was certainly a cold-weather soup—but maybe, just maybe, a tiny part of her was thinking, *And if he doesn't like it, he can make himself a sandwich.*

He could also stay away from the soup group altogether if he wanted to, honestly. The group joked about Ron's enjoying the benefits of membership without ever cooking soup himself, but there was an uncomfortable grain of truth in the jokes.

Yes, he provided the wine. But wine wasn't soup—it wasn't an act of creation, no matter how carefully chosen it was to complement the meal.

Alicia pulled the stirring spoon out, blew on it, and tasted. Oh man, it was good. The mustard was just right; the Worcestershire sauce gave it an interesting tang; the cheese hadn't broken or curdled, but stayed perfectly creamy. The whole effect was thick and rich without being cloying. Alicia smiled. Yes, Steph was their gourmet cook, but everyone enjoyed the challenge of coming up with new and interesting soups.

Last meeting, at Julie's house, had been spectacular. They'd enjoyed a mushroom feast inspired by a meal Julie's daughters had cooked before they both went back home to Portland: cream of morel soup from Julie, shiitake mushroom pizzas from Steph, a gruyère and mushroom tart that Lynne had brought. And all the mushrooms had been locally sourced.

Ron of course had griped about the dangers of eating wild mushrooms, but he'd gobbled up at least his fair share of the bounty if not more, and then fallen all over himself praising Steph for her pizzas.

Seemed like the only time he ever said anything nice to or about anyone, Steph was involved.

Good luck with that, old man, Alicia thought, rolling her eyes as she went over to the back counter for the loaf of french bread. She carved the loaf into thick slices before reheating the two big skillets on the stove. Then she checked the recipe again—oops, it said to sprinkle them with red wine before frying them in the butter that the onion had cooked in. Okay, well, olive oil, supposedly; but she'd used butter, because come on. Cheese soup? Of course it wanted butter.

There was a bottle of red wine open on the island, with its excess air removed before its special preserving cork had been put in last night. It was something French; Alicia hadn't wanted more than a glass last night, and Ron hadn't wanted to drink the remainder of the bottle himself. Would he mind if she used a splash of it for cooking?

Who was she kidding? Of course he would. She wouldn't put it past him to have measured the level in the bottle before he went to bed last night, and recorded it in one of his little logbooks somewhere.

So, her options were: she could go to his study, knock on the door, disturbing him from whatever vitally important intellectual work he was undoubtedly doing in there, and ask him for some cooking wine. She could go to the basement and try to figure out something suitable for cooking with, without his input. Or, she could use a few sprinkles of the wine that was *right here* when she needed it.

If you wanted to keep it safe from being used in the cooking, you could have put it somewhere besides the kitchen island, she thought, pulling out the cork.

By the time Ron realized what she had done, the guests had already started arriving, so he had to rein in his complaints, keeping them down to something like his usual dull roar. Alicia almost didn't notice her friends' glances anymore, whenever Ron said something particularly sour. *Yes, I know*, she thought, as he muttered and grumbled. *Professors should never be allowed to retire.*

Now, Ron sulked over by the windows while Julie and Steph sat at the bar, glasses of wine in front of them (*not* the French stuff; something else Ron had produced from his vast collection, of course). Lynne was driving separately tonight, as she was coming from a meeting at the health clinic in town; Matt had texted that he was running a little bit late, but that he would get there as soon as he could, and they should start eating without him if they needed to.

"This is gorgeous," Steph said, looking over the notebook Alicia had set before her two friends. "Your calligraphy is perfect."

"Seriously, it is," Julie put in. "I was already excited about this project, but now I cannot *wait* to get it put together."

Alicia laughed as she tore lettuce leaves for the salad. "Well, I'm afraid you will have to wait at least a little while; calligraphy isn't a fast art."

"How long did it take you to write out this one recipe?" Steph asked.

"Oh, maybe two hours. But I'll get faster as I go along—I'm a little rusty, and I was also playing around with the layout a bit."

Julie frowned. "Two hours? Yikes. If we have a hundred recipes in the book, this is going to represent a huge time commitment for you."

"Not to mention the editing," Steph added, glancing back at Ron.

The doorbell rang, and Lynne let herself in. "Wow, smells great in here!" She came over to the island and set down a square box. "Cardamom snickerdoodles from the bread bakery—oh good," she added, noticing what Alicia was doing, "you're already making a salad."

"I knew you weren't going to get back home after your meeting," Alicia said. "This just made more sense."

"Do you want help?"

"No, I've got it. My soup is done, and the bread is keeping warm in the oven."

Ron came over and poured Lynne a glass of wine, and refilled his own, which he had emptied in record time. Fortunately, it seemed to have mellowed him out a bit. He took a stool next to Steph, shoving over a pile of mail in order to make room for his glass.

"Oh, Julie, is that measure on the ballot something to do with your parking meter thing?" Alicia asked, glancing at the mail.

"There's a ballot?" Julie asked. "I haven't gotten anything."

"Yeah, they came today," Alicia said. "Or I guess yesterday—I didn't get out to the mailbox till today though."

"Don't the pamphlets usually come first?" Julie asked.

Alicia shrugged. "There's just one measure on the ballot—the pamphlet came with it, just a little folded thing. I think it's on the coffee table if you want to look at it."

"What's on for this election?" Lynne asked.

"There shouldn't be anything—it's too soon for a primary," Julie said with a frown, getting down from her stool and retrieving the ballot pamphlet. "This is it? It's barely a flier."

"Yeah, that's it."

Julie came back and unfolded it. Then her eyes widened. "Oh, now wait just a minute…"

"What is it?" Steph asked, leaning over to see. "What's a Special Purpose District?"

"I'm not entirely sure," Julie said, now sounding angry, "but I have a terrible feeling about this. I was told there wouldn't be any election till April at the earliest. This is, like, practically next *week*."

Ron leaned in to try and see as well. "*Is* it about the parking meters?"

"It doesn't say anything about them, at least in the summary," Julie said. "In fact the whole thing is suspiciously vague, if you ask me."

The door opened and in came Matt. "Sorry, everyone," he said, shrugging out of his jacket and setting a covered dish on the counter. "Dad was kind of having a moment, so I wanted to stick around and make sure he was going to be okay to leave with Ramona for a few hours." Then he noticed what everyone was doing. "What's up?"

Julie looked up at him, clearly furious. "I need to find the whole text of the measure, but I think that stinker McLeod made an end run around us."

"He did? Well, I'll just call the judge again—"

Julie shook her head and lifted up the pamphlet. "There's a measure on the ballot—the only one, a whole special election just for this."

"Wait, what?" Matt asked. "There's an election?"

"Yeah," Julie said. "With one item on it: a measure to create a Special Purpose Tax District in the downtown business area of Eastsound to 'preserve its historic character.'"

Matt looked confused, and so did everyone else, Alicia thought. "That sounds like a good thing, doesn't it?" he asked.

"It sure does!" Julie, fuming, stabbed her index finger at the pamphlet. "And it's complete bullshit—totally dishonest. He's

using our language against us. Everyone who came to the meetings or signed the petitions is going to think this is *our* measure.
But look—see, here?" She pointed. "This Special Purpose Tax
District comes with a budget for signs, administration, and en-
forcement, and the budget is to be raised entirely from 'direct
community-based revenue mechanisms'!" She blew out a breath.
"Wow, I knew that guy was a jerk, but I didn't imagine he'd go
this far."

"I'm still not quite getting it," Lynne said. "Are you sure this is
for parking meters?"

"It has to be." Julie got up and paced across the room, her
agitation visible. "I have to call Gavin, see what he knows about
this. Unbelievable." She walked back over to her purse and dug
in it for her cell phone, then strode over to the windows where
the signal was better.

"Let me see that," Ron said, picking up the ballot pamphlet
and looking at it. "Is this all that came? This is just a summary."

Everyone else glanced at each other, a little mystified. "Maybe we can find the full text online?" Matt said, pulling out his
phone.

Alicia opened the oven and checked on the bread, which wow,
smelled really good. "I think we can eat anytime," she told the
group. "As soon as Julie's off the phone."

"Need help carrying anything to the table?" Steph asked, taking a sip of her wine before getting up.

"Yeah—the salad, and Matt's veggie dish. But let's build the
soup bowls here." Alicia pulled out the bread, set it on the stove,
and got bowls out of the cupboard by the sink. "Start with a
piece of toast, and ladle however much soup you want over it. I'll
demonstrate."

"Is this Welsh rarebit?" Steph asked, looking amazed, in a good
way. "But as a soup?"

"Exactly!" Alicia said, feeling proud. "The ultimate winter
soup."

Ron frowned and set the pamphlet down. "She might be right. If so, this is really sneaky. Everyone's going to think this is the result of all the community effort, when instead it's just the opposite."

Julie walked back to the group, stuffing her phone in her pocket. "He's going to get hold of Leslie Magnas and see what we can do." She frowned. "It's too late to prevent it from getting on the ballot, obviously, so our only recourse is to work as hard as we can to get the word out about what's going on here, and make sure everyone votes against this."

"How did we not know this was coming?" Matt asked, ladling soup over his toast. "Wow, Alicia, this smells killer."

"Thanks." She smiled at him.

"The man clearly had several different efforts going concurrently," Julie said, shaking her head. "In fact, I wonder if that's an avenue we could pursue…I'm pretty sure that all those fresh-faced teenagers carrying clipboards around town last fall weren't collecting signatures for this measure. So how did it even get approved for the ballot?"

"By a resolution of the county council, voted on in December," Matt said, reading from his phone.

"The county council!" Julie exclaimed. "Where Orcas has *one* member." She shook her head. "No fair, letting Lopez and San Juan decide such important issues about our village."

"Anyway," Matt went on, "I found the full text of the measure as well, on the county website—I'll send you the link."

"Hey, everyone, let's eat before it gets cold," Alicia said. "Anyone who doesn't have a bowl, grab one and get yourself set up!"

In a few minutes, they were at the table, and the conversation refocused on the meal. Alicia was relieved that Julie seemed to get herself together and was enjoying the meal, but she felt particularly gratified to see Steph digging into her bowl with gusto. In fact, Steph looked fantastic—bright-eyed, cheerful, energetic. She was always an attractive woman, but tonight she seemed even more luminous than usual.

"This definitely goes in the cookbook," Steph said, scraping her empty bowl. "That was astonishing. I would have never thought of making Welsh rarebit as a soup."

Alicia wanted to wiggle with delight. Across the table, she caught Ron's eye. *See?* she thought. *I can do something right.*

He looked away from her. "I'll be right back," he announced to the table, pushing back his chair and heading down to the wine cellar.

STEPH

SINCE LYNNE AND she had driven separately tonight, Steph was careful about her alcohol intake, not wanting to drive the dark island roads with any bit of a buzz on.

But honestly, as exceptional as Ron's wines always were, she felt almost no need for a drink at the moment. She and David had been in a state of heightened bliss ever since the "date night" and their return to lovemaking...she felt pleasantly drunk half the time, even when she'd had nothing stronger than coffee.

Ah, endorphins.

How in the world did I let things go so long without saying something? she asked herself, as she turned left out of Eastsound and started down Orcas Road. Of course, she knew the answer: it was the classic frog-in-the-pot syndrome, where each tiny increment of separation between them—being busy, being tired, wanting to finish that one last piece of work, taking each other for granted, feeling introverted—had just been another snowflake (to scramble metaphors), building toward the eventual catastrophe of an avalanche.

But the avalanche hadn't come, because it had literally snowed instead, and David had had to rejoin Steph in their marriage bed, and now suddenly all was well.

She hummed along with the music playing as she drove, looking forward to getting home and telling him about her evening. He had promised to wait up for her; had even seemed as though he was looking forward to it.

Sure enough, in addition to the porch lights she saw when she pulled into their driveway, she saw the warm glow of living room lights.

They'd been enjoying a fire most evenings, though not always making love in front of it; it had quickly become a cherished routine, an end-of-the-day tradition.

"Hi honey I'm home!" Steph called out as she walked in.

"I'm in here," he called back, from the direction of the living room.

She smiled as she joined him, seeing two snifters of brandy on the low table before him. "Oh good; I hardly touched Sommelier Ron's wine tonight." She sat on the couch next to David, leaning in to give him a slow kiss. "Brandy is the perfect thing right now, thank you."

He raised his snifter; she clinked with hers, then they both sipped. "Ooh, you warmed it," she said, smiling at him.

"You taught me that."

"This is heated just right. How did you know exactly when I'd be home?"

He shrugged, smiling back at her. "Just lucky, I guess." At her look, he laughed. "Okay, I warmed them a while ago, and then I held your glass in my hands to keep it warm, but then I went and reheated it a few minutes ago. If you'd been much later, I'd have had to do it again."

"Am I late?"

"No—you're right in the middle of the range of time when you said you'd be home."

"That's what I thought." She toed off her shoes and put her stockinged feet up on the coffee table. "Did you have a nice evening?"

He sipped his brandy. "Yes. It was fine."

"What did you eat?"

"I heated up the pasta you left me. It was good."

She glanced at him. "Did you eat in your study?"

He gave a soft laugh. "No. I ate dinner in the dining room like a civilized person, and then I've been reading in here."

"Nice." She looked around, not seeing a book, or even any magazines other than her various cooking ones. His phone wasn't on the coffee table, either. "What are you reading?"

Now he looked abashed. "Ah, you don't want to know."

"David," she said softly. "I never told you not to read your market stuff. I never even told you not to work—I just asked you to have dinner with me more often."

He shrugged again. "Well, you didn't have to tell me not to work. I could see how unhealthy and obsessive I've gotten about it all—and unfair to you, too—once you brought it up. So I'm trying to wean off…very slowly, though."

"And that's just fine. *We're* fine." Because they were. She sipped her brandy and leaned against him, relaxing into his warmth as the drink warmed her from the inside. She tried to inhale his familiar scent, but couldn't detect it over the brandy.

"How was the meeting?" David asked, after a minute. "Did you have fun?"

"I did. Alicia made the most amazing soup ever—it was actually very creative, and completely delicious. And we talked more about the cookbook idea. She did some hand-lettering of one of the recipes, which came out really well." Then she frowned. "Oh, but before that, there was something about the parking meter thing. Did our ballots come?"

"Yes, they did; they're in your study. Do you want me to get them?"

"Not right now—I want to drink this and go to bed, I'm pretty wiped. But we should look at them tomorrow. Apparently, that developer guy or whoever he is did a dirty trick on everyone, and he's got a measure on the ballot to create a whole tax agency or something. And he did it so deceptively that Julie's worried people are going to vote for it, thinking it's what *her* group was pushing for." She shook her head. "I don't completely understand it all, but it sounds sneaky and underhanded, and I'll bet there are going to be some more community meetings before too long."

David shivered next to her. "Ugh, meetings."

Steph laughed. "Don't worry. I won't make you go to any meetings."

They finished their brandies and went to bed together, where Steph found that, tired though she was, she wasn't too tired to reach out for him in the dark.

MATT

NOT LONG AFTER he left Alicia and Ron's house, Matt's phone dinged with a text. He looked for a place to pull over and see who it was—with his dad the way he was at the moment, he didn't want to miss an alert from Ramona.

He passed a few driveways, but didn't feel right about blocking them, so he ended up waiting till the wide spot in the road that led to the cutoff for the top of Mount Constitution, in Moran State Park. He parked and pulled out his phone.

It was from Julie's daughter Megan. Matt smiled, in both simple relief and...the other, more complicated emotion.

Hope your meeting was "souper" tonight! ;)

Despite himself, Matt chuckled. He started to type out a response, then stopped, pulled out his earbuds and slipped them in, and phoned her.

She answered after one ring. "Get it? Souper?"

"Yes, same as two weeks ago," he said, laughing, as he pulled back onto the road. "You know, jokes aren't funny if you keep telling the same ones over and over."

"Oh, I beg to differ," she said. "I personally think it gets funnier every time. Repetition, you know: one of the pillars of humor."

"It's also gauche to laugh at your own jokes."

"Again we disagree!" she said, starting to laugh herself. "My goodness, we're going to be hopeless as friends, aren't we?"

"Entirely hopeless. We should cease communicating instantly."

Matt had felt a blinding surge of attraction to Megan the night he'd met her, at Steph's Christmas party; the attraction had seemed like it might be mutual.

They'd managed to have three outings together—Matt hesitated to call them dates—before she and her sister had returned to Portland after the new year. They'd hit it off beautifully, with a comfortable rapport (despite the terrible jokes); she was so easy to talk to. Warm, cheerful, empathetic. Yet both he and, he thought, she had held back during their first outing, a cup of coffee at the little café in the back of Darvill's Bookstore. They'd gotten a bit more personal during their second meeting, a crisp but breezy walk along Crescent Beach; not until their third get-together, over tall draft IPAs at the Lower Tavern two nights before she went home, did they overtly discuss "this thing," as Megan put it, gesturing between them.

Sadly but wisely, they'd decided that the "thing" was not in the cards for them, at least for now. Matt was still recovering from Heather's abrupt departure, and most of his free time was taken up by his father's needs. And, well, Megan lived in Portland. She had a life there, a sister and a close group of friends, as well as a job which, though she didn't love it, was important to her.

Yes, her mother lived here on Orcas, and Megan did visit her regularly. But would visits be enough, if they wanted to explore a real relationship? Matt had no great desire for a long-distance romance. He'd rarely seen them work out, even with people who were far less distracted and overcommitted than he was. Honestly, even if he were dating someone who lived on the island, Matt didn't have much to offer a partner right now.

He also couldn't see himself moving to Portland. His business was established here; he owned his house; and uprooting his father was definitely not something to be undertaken lightly, if at all. Besides, he loved it here. Orcas was home.

So, over those beers at the Lower, they had decided to be friends, and to make no guesses about the future one way or the other.

"Instantly," she agreed now. "In fact I'm hanging up this very moment, and deleting your number." She paused for a half a second. "Did I hang up?"

"You don't seem to have," Matt said. "Though I should warn you, if it sounds like I hung up, it's only because I'm driving and the call dropped."

"So how was the dinner?" she asked, as her giggles finally wound down. "As yummy and wine-soaked as usual?"

"Pretty darn yummy," Matt said. "Though you should call your mom—apparently that parking meter thing has taken an unexpected turn."

"Oh no! What happened?"

"There's a measure on the ballot that's being voted on next week, and it looks like that vacation rental guy managed to make it sound like it will do just the opposite of what it really will do. It's all about 'preserve our local character' or whatever, but it's really going to set up some kind of commission or tax district or something. I'm not clear on the details."

"I'll call my mom as soon as we hang up. Oh, she must be furious."

"You know it!" Matt was driving through town now, about to turn right on Lover's Lane. "Actually, I'm going to be home in a few minutes here, which means she's probably just getting home as well. Do you want to try and chat tomorrow?"

"Sure, that would be great. Are you going get all busy doing more meetings and whatnot? You don't have much time if the election is next week—does that mean Tuesday?"

"A week from Tuesday, and no, I don't think I'm going to have as much time at the moment. My dad had another little scene right when I was leaving for dinner this evening."

"Oh, I'm so sorry," Megan said. "I'll let you go, and good luck. We'll talk tomorrow."

"Bye."

He took the turn up Enchanted Forest Road, feeling the mixture of warmth and longing that always stayed with him after he talked with Megan. Or even when he just thought about her, as he did many times a day. Time and distance—and their very mature and responsible decision to just be friends—had not diminished his strong feelings for her.

It was nice of her to reach out, even if it was with the same bad pun as two weeks ago. He hoped she'd get hold of her mother; Julie had been really upset this evening.

Matt did feel bad that he wasn't going to be able to be more help with the sudden emergency community organizing that Julie and Gavin would no doubt be doing over the next week or so, but Gordon's dementia had recently made a shift. Matt didn't know if this was temporary or the new normal; he, and to some degree Ramona, had to figure out how to deal with it.

Gordon had always been a cheerful, social man, and at first, his memory loss hadn't impacted that at all. If anything, it had made him even more gregarious, delighted to see and interact with people, even if he didn't remember who they were. Starting around the new year, though, he'd been subject to episodes of gloominess, almost depression; a listless hopelessness and a pronounced lack of energy. "I think this is going to be my last new year," he'd said on New Year's Day.

"Oh, you don't know that," Matt had said, laughing it off. Not thinking anything more of it, until one morning a few days later when Gordon had slept in unusually late, and then sort of dragged around all day, not wanting to do any of his usual activities. Not even wanting to eat.

Matt had persuaded his father to at least take a little food and drink, which had perked Gordon up at least to the point where it seemed like everything was fine again. *He was probably dehydrated*, Matt thought. So many seniors, even ones without cognitive issues, didn't drink enough water.

He had sort of bounced around between seeming himself and not-himself since then. This evening, as Matt was about to leave for soup group at Ron and Alicia's, Gordon had again been low, nearly despondent—and cranky as well.

"Ramona will be here in a few minutes," Matt had told his dad, after waking him up from where he was dozing in the recliner.

"I'm going to bed," Gordon had said, after blinking confusedly. "Tell her she doesn't need to come."

"Dad, she's already on her way, and I cannot leave you alone for the evening, even if you're just sleeping. You know that."

Gordon had scowled. "It's a waste of money, paying her to babysit me."

"You have plenty of money. And you like Ramona; she's been looking forward to seeing you." *Not to mention she relies on this money*, Matt thought. He'd pull out those big guns only if he needed to.

"What's she gonna do if I croak? She's not a nurse."

Matt had gazed down at his father, trying to figure out what to say. "Do you think you're going to croak?" he finally asked.

"I just want to go to bed." Gordon had pushed the button to un-recline the chair, gotten up, and shuffled off toward his room; Matt had followed him.

"You haven't had dinner," Matt had said. "Do you want to try to eat a little something?"

"I'm not your child. Quit nagging me—I'll eat when I'm hungry." His dad went into his bathroom and shut the door. Matt had been unable to persuade him to even stay up long enough to say hi to Ramona.

When she did arrive, they'd discussed the issue.

"Do you think I should call the doctor?" he'd asked her.

"Not on a Sunday night," she'd said. "It doesn't seem like an emergency. But this has been going on for a while, and you're right, this is not like him."

"I mean, if ever there was a reason to be depressed, this would be it," Matt had said. "All he's facing for the rest of his life is losing things: his memory, people he loves, his autonomy, and then eventually himself."

"I do think a non-emergency visit to the doctor is a good idea at this point. When was his last blood work done?"

"I'd have to look it up," Matt said. "Maybe six months ago? Something like that."

"It could be a medication thing. Something out of balance."

"Yeah. I'll call and get him an appointment tomorrow."

Matt now turned off onto their little private road, and parked in front of the house, next to Ramona's truck. When he let himself in, he found Ramona in the living room, reading a book in the recliner.

"Oh, you're back already!" she said, sitting up.

He smiled. "I'm not early. What are you reading?"

"Just a novel—I guess I got caught up in it and lost track of time." She tucked it into her big purse beside the chair.

He sat on the sofa next to the recliner. "How did it go this evening?"

Ramona frowned slightly. "Fine, more or less; I did go in and check on him, and he was awake. So I convinced him to get up and join me in the living room for a little while."

"That's great! Did he eat anything?"

She shook her head. "No, but he drank some orange juice. We watched a game show, and then he wanted to go back to bed. I tried to convince him to watch the news with me, but he said it was all bad news and it would be just the same tomorrow so why bother."

Matt frowned, leaning forward to rest his chin in his hands. "Yeah. I definitely will call the clinic tomorrow and see if we can figure out what's up with him."

"I was thinking more about it after you left," Ramona said. "It could just be a bad case of the winter blues. I've been reading more studies about seniors—with and without dementia—being even more heavily impacted by incorrect light than younger people."

"Incorrect light?"

"For their circadian rhythms." Ramona gave him a self-deprecating smile. "I know, you didn't know I was a biological research fan, right? But there's all this interesting work being done in the field of light and health—how we're supposed to get bright days and dark nights, and yet we get just the opposite. Anyway, it impacts seniors very strongly, messing with their sleep and their cognitive health. And it's particularly a problem for us up here in the far north."

"Huh." This was the first Matt had heard of any of this, but it did make sense. Certainly worth asking Gordon's doctor about.

"Your dad probably doesn't get a lick of natural daylight these days," Ramona said. "I notice he likes to keep the shades pulled, when I'm here in the daytime."

"He says the light hurts his eyes," Matt said. "And he likes his privacy, no matter how many times I explain to him that nobody but deer and raccoons are here on the property ready to peer in the windows."

Ramona nodded, with a wry smile. "And then he watches TV in the evenings. There's probably not much you can do here in February, but when spring comes, you might want to see if he'll sit outside in the daytime some. Especially in the mornings."

"I will see what I can do. He hates being outside—says it's too cold. You'd never know he grew up in Minnesota."

"I definitely feel the cold more than I used to when I was younger," Ramona said, getting up out of the recliner. "Anyway, I'd best be off. I hope you had a nice evening?"

"It was good, thanks. I was a little distracted worrying about him, but I knew you'd call me if I needed to know anything, or to get back here."

"That's right, I absolutely would." She patted him on the shoulder as she headed out to the front hall for her coat.

After she left, Matt felt tired but not sleepy. It was only a little after nine; in the olden days, he and Heather would have maybe started a movie, even if she would usually fall asleep before the film was halfway over.

He didn't feel like watching a movie alone.

He went down the hall and peeked into his dad's room. Gordon was asleep, snoring softly, curled on his right side. Matt closed the bedroom door and went into the kitchen. He washed the dish he'd brought the broccoli gratin in and put it in the dish drain. He opened the fridge, looked at all the food he was too full to eat, and closed it again. He opened the liquor cabinet, stared at the bottles of things he wasn't interested in drinking, and closed it again.

Back in the living room, he pulled out his cell phone and stared at it. Megan's text was the last thing that had come in. What he really wanted to do was call her. But it was too late for that, and they'd already talked this evening, not even a half-hour ago, and they were going to talk tomorrow. He should probably wait until he'd called the clinic to call her, so he could give her at least that much of an update.

People who were *just friends* did not talk on the phone several times a day. People who were *just friends* did not call each other late at night when they were in lonely despair. People who were *just friends* maintained a reasonable emotional distance from each other.

Matt gazed across the empty living room for a while, then got up, turned out all the lights, brushed his teeth, and went to bed.

STEPH

DAVID SLEPT. STEPH lay awake beside him.

She wished she could turn on a light and read. She had been sleeping better since they'd gotten used to sharing a bed again, but not perfectly. Should she get up and go read in her study? But she didn't want to leave this warmth and coziness.

Their lovemaking tonight had been…nice, but not electric. Well of course it hadn't been electric! They'd been together for decades. It wasn't *supposed* to be electric. It was supposed to be loving, and comforting, and sweet. Familiar.

It had just been extra-hot when they had started up again after so long. Of course that level of passion was never going to last.

This was fine. This was totally fine—more than fine, it was great.

Was he retreating? He had seemed…not entirely present tonight, and not just after they got into bed. Was he just embarrassed about kinda-sorta working while she had been at soup group? But she didn't care about that. She wasn't trying to control his life. He must know that.

Was it something about the soup group itself? He'd seemed cheerful enough before she'd headed out for the evening, though still insisting he had no interest in coming along.

Was the depression making inroads again? As nice as their wine dinners and brandy after-dinners were, maybe she shouldn't encourage so much drinking. It had never seemed to affect his moods all that much; he seemed able to take it or leave it, enjoying a glass or two with her, never using it as a crutch or an escape. But she knew there was a strong correlation between alcohol use and depression in many people.

Well, she'd think about it, and keep an eye on him. And she'd ask him about it if he didn't seem better in the next day or two.

Beside her, he sighed softly in his sleep.

Chapter 4

JULIE

On Tuesday, Julie was supposed to get together with Alicia and Steph for lunch, to discuss the next steps on the cookbook. She texted them both that morning.

I don't know if I can make it, guys, she wrote. *Gavin and I are going out to Island Cottages this morning to meet with Leslie about getting an emergency community meeting set up. I'm not sure how long it will take.*

You're meeting about a meeting? Alicia texted back, with a winky emoji. *No worries, Jules—we can push this back a week, or even two weeks.*

Steph chimed in: *Alicia, let's still get together as planned. Julie, you can join us if your meeting gets done in time, but if not, I think we still have plenty of things we can cover, and run them by you later.*

Sounds good, Alicia wrote.

Julie sent a thumbs-up.

Gavin appeared at her door a few minutes later. Julie opened it at his knock. "You can just let yourself in, you know," she said, pulling him close for a sweet kiss. "It's never locked."

"I know. But I like this." He ran his arms down her back and leaned into her, kissing her again. "If I just walked in, I'd have to go and find you to get my kiss. And what if you were busy? Then what would I do?"

She laughed, some of the tension that had her shoulders up around her ears easing. "Never too busy to kiss you," she said, and demonstrated.

A few minutes later, still in the open doorway, Gavin pulled back and said, "We should probably..."

"Yeah, I know." She smiled ruefully. "Leslie's waiting, blah blah blah. Come in for a second—I need to put something warmer on. Since I can't wrap you around me while we're meeting with Leslie."

"True," he said, seeming to consider it. "Unfortunate, but true."

The day, though brightly sunny for a nice change, was crisp and cold. She drove them out toward West Sound and the vacation rental cottages that Leslie owned and managed. "It seems ironic to me," Julie said, as they passed the big open fields in Crow Valley, "that our nemesis makes his living renting to tourists, and so does our strongest ally."

"It's a funny coincidence, but not all that improbable, I think," Gavin said. "Orcas Island's economy depends on tourism—at least these days. You also sell to tourists."

"And to locals," she said, then laughed. "I mean, not to sound defensive or anything. You're absolutely right." She thought a moment. "I guess the ironic part, to me, is that I feel like we should all be on the same team. What even is Sam McLeod trying to accomplish, by alienating local business owners? And, for that matter, does he really think tourists are going to enjoy feeding quarters—or their credit cards—into parking meters?"

"I assume he thinks they won't notice, or won't care," Gavin said. "You can't park anywhere in downtown Seattle for free. And you certainly can't travel to the islands for free. Maybe he thinks that after spending ninety dollars to bring their car and family here, another buck or two for parking will be nothing to them."

"Hmph."

"But as for alienating local business owners—your guess is as good as mine."

"Some people know what's best for everyone," she said, rolling her eyes. "Despite all evidence to the contrary."

"True."

She drove on, turning at the little marina, and then following the shoreline a half-mile or so till they reached the Island Cottages' driveway. She parked in front of the tiny office; Leslie stepped out to meet them.

"I'd hoped we could sit out in this nice sunshine and have coffee, but it's too cold," she said. "Come on in."

"Windy, too," Gavin pointed out, grabbing for his fisherman's cap before it blew off his head and into the sound.

Inside Leslie's office cottage, they sat around a low table and drank small cups of weak coffee. Julie could see the big old-fashioned restaurant-style coffee maker behind Leslie's desk, with a big box of Rykoff Sexton coffee packs beside it. At least she served them real half-and-half, not the powdered stuff. But the whole establishment had a Been Here Forever; This Was Good Enough For My Folks So Why Should I Change Anything vibe.

Charming, though, in its old island way. Julie hadn't ever been out here before, but she got the strong sense that this was the kind of place that visitors returned to every year—renting the same cottage for the same week, bringing the same family members, meeting up with the same friends who rented the same neighboring cottages. She'd bet anything there was a big bonfire setup down on the beach, and, in the summertime, a shack that sold corn dogs and ice cream, plus wine and beer to the grownups.

"All right," said Leslie, once they were all settled, "I did get hold of Judge Varela, just in case. And you're right: this was all done legally, so there's nothing we can do about that."

"Sneaky, though," Gavin said.

"Very sneaky. But legal." Leslie shook her head. "So we have basically a week to get the word out to the voters. I say we go straight back to the channels we used before—get hold of the Odd Fellows and see if we can have another meeting there, find anyone who's willing to host small meetings—"

"Wait a second," Julie said. They both turned to her. "What about the 'arguments in favor' and 'arguments opposed' to the measure? Who wrote the argument opposed to this thing? I didn't notice."

Leslie got up and went back to her desk, rummaged around a bit, and brought a ballot pamphlet back to the table. "Huh," she snorted. "Says there wasn't one submitted in opposition."

"Because nobody knew there was anything there to be opposed to," Gavin said, looking disgusted.

"That might be a point to explore." Leslie made a note in the margin of the pamphlet. "I'll follow up with the judge, see if proper legal notice was given."

"Who wrote the argument in favor?" Julie asked.

Leslie handed her the pamphlet.

Julie skimmed the bland, uninformative argument, then looked at the authors' names. "Who are these people? None of them are Sam McLeod."

"He wouldn't put his name on this," Leslie said, looking at least as disgusted as Gavin did. "Anyway, I don't know who any of those folks are either. 'Local business owner,' it says after each one, but I don't recognize those names."

"You'd think they'd put the names of their businesses on here, at least," Julie said. "Something smells funny about all of this."

"It doesn't matter, though," Leslie said, "at least not right now. If we can get this measure defeated, then we won't care who he finagled into putting their names on it—whether these people even exist. So that's where we need to focus our efforts: voter outreach."

"Mostly about getting people to actually vote," Gavin said. "Turnout is always super low in small elections."

"Yeah," Leslie agreed. "I wonder how many people are even

around this time of year."

Ugh, that's right, Julie thought. Even many of the island's so-called year-round residents vacationed in warmer places in the winter. "Well, all we can do is try," she said.

"I'm calling the Odd Fellows right now," Gavin said, pulling out his phone.

"And I'll start calling the people who hosted small meetings last fall," Julie added.

Leslie nodded. "That's a big list: let's split it up." She got up again and went to her desk, returning with a printed out spreadsheet. "Here—we can go over this and divvy up the names."

Someone obviously picked up at the other end of the line with Gavin; he stood up and walked out of the tiny cottage, having his conversation on the porch. He returned a minute later. "Okay, we're in for a meeting Thursday at six."

"Perfect," Julie said. "If we can get fliers made today, I can help distribute them around town."

"Too bad there isn't time to get anything out in the mail to every registered voter," Leslie said.

"He was counting on catching us with our pants down," Gavin said, looking fierce and, in Julie's entirely unbiased opinion, terribly sexy as a result. Or maybe it was just the unexpected image brought on by the phrase *with our pants down*. "We'll just have to show him what we're made of."

They spent a little time going over Leslie's list, agreeing who would make which calls, and then complaining once more about how sneaky and unfair this whole situation was. When Leslie offered them a second cup of coffee, though, they both refused. "I have to get to the library," Gavin said.

"Well, thanks for coming all the way out here," Leslie said to them both.

"It was our pleasure," Julie said. "You shouldn't always have to be the one driving to meet us. And I was curious to see your cottages—this whole place is so cute."

"I'd be happy to give you a tour if you have time."

Julie glanced at Gavin, who shook his head sadly. "No, I really do have to get to work," he told them both. "I got permission to come in two hours late, which we can just make if we leave now."

On their way back to town, Gavin said to Julie, "You still have time to meet your friends for lunch if you want."

"I don't know, I feel like I should get started on those phone calls."

"It's up to you." Gavin shrugged. "But you do have to eat, right?"

She laughed, without much humor. "Are you trying to get rid of me?"

"Not at all," he said, smiling back at her. "You'll be getting rid of me—unless you want to spend the day at the library watching me work."

"Tempting as that sounds…" she started, trailing off meaningfully.

He nodded. "Exactly. So go to your lunch, if you want. I don't want you dropping everything that's important to you to take care of this stuff."

"This stuff?" She glanced over at him. "I know you brought me into this, but it's very important to me. It impacts my business—my whole livelihood. And the community I live in."

Gavin reached over and took her hand in his; she squeezed it, then let go, putting her hand back on the wheel. "I do know that," he said. "I guess I'm just making sure you're not sacrificing more than you intended to."

"Well, none of us wanted any of this to be happening," she pointed out. "But now that it is, I'm all in to help with it." She thought another moment. "Though you're right: I do need to eat. And I'll probably have better luck getting hold of people in the evening. Assuming anyone's even around, as Leslie said."

After she dropped him off at the library, she parked in front of her shop and pulled out her phone, opening the text string with

Steph and Alicia.

You guys still at Ladybug?

We are! Steph texted back a minute later. *Are you done meeting about meeting?*

I am, and I'm hungry, and need to get the taste of institutional coffee out of my mouth. I'll be right there.

In the pizza place, Julie ordered a slice of pepperoni at the counter, debated whether to add a glass of red wine, and ultimately just asked for water. Then she joined her friends at their table.

"How did it go?" Alicia asked.

Julie filled them in, around bites of delicious pizza. They expressed the appropriate amount of indignation and made offers to help in whatever way they could, but Julie knew this issue didn't affect either of them anywhere near as much as it did her. "Thanks," she told them. "Just get the word around as best you can, like you did before."

"Do you want us to come to Thursday's meeting?" Steph asked.

"If you want to—but you don't need to. It's more to let people know what's happening, and since you already know, it might not be the best use of your time." She looked at the notebooks on the table, stacked next to greasy paper plates. "So, did I miss the cookbook meeting? Are you guys all ready to publish now?"

They both laughed. "Not at all," Alicia said. "Steph was trying to figure out how to save me from working ten million hours on hand-lettering."

"I'm just saying," Steph said. "There are beautiful calligraphy fonts!"

"And they look like fonts drawn by a computer," Alicia said. "I really don't mind doing this, honestly. And aren't we all still thinking about a kind of original Moosewood Cookbook feel?"

"With hand-drawn illustrations too?" Julie asked, leaning forward. "Ooh, I wonder if Lori would be interested in helping out."

"She draws?" Steph asked. "I thought she was a sculptor."

"Apparently every artist draws, or at least knows how," Julie said. "Or so I'm told."

Alicia shrugged. "I wouldn't know. Calligraphy is as far as I ever got with visual arts, before I realized that editing was really my thing."

They talked a bit more about the cookbook, agreeing to meet again in a few weeks, after Alicia had lettered more recipes and kept track of her time.

"I don't know about you all," Steph said, "but I'm going to get another slice."

Alicia looked at her thoughtfully for a moment. Then she shrugged. "You know what? That's an awesome idea."

"Well, far be it from me to be the odd one out," Julie said.

When they were back at their table with new hot slices, Steph said to Julie, "So, community crises aside, how are you doing? You look great—very happy. Things still good with Gavin?"

"So good," Julie said, smiling broadly, then wiping pizza sauce off her chin. "He's wonderful." Then she chuckled. "Are you guys both sure you don't want to start another book group? He's really serious about getting one going, and I've really missed having one."

"I just don't read a lot of fiction," Steph said. "Whenever I'm in a book group, that ends up being the only book I read that month, and it's usually not something I would have chosen. So then it starts feeling like homework."

"Same here, in a way," Alicia said. "For me, reading *is* homework—it's my work. I enjoy it, but reading and analyzing and discussing something doesn't feel like a leisure activity. Not like making soup—or just reading a book for fun and not having to think about it after I put it down."

"You'll find a few people," Steph assured her. "Your man works in a *library*, after all. Surely he runs into readers there?"

"Well, yeah," Julie admitted. "But those are strangers. I want to be in a book group with my friends."

"We were all strangers before you started the first book group," Alicia pointed out.

"And now we're soup buddies!" Steph said.

"Soup and everything else buddies," Alicia put in, looking warmly at Steph.

Julie grinned at both of them. These were indeed among her best friends—and not just on the island, but anywhere. "Steph," she said, "since you asked me, how are *you* doing? You look happy as well."

Steph smiled. "I am. David and I…" She trailed off, looking suddenly shy, which was so unlike Steph that both Julie and Alicia just stared at her. "We're in a good place right now. Since the Christmas party, when you were all snowed in and stayed at our house, and he had to sleep in my bed…he's still sleeping there." Her cheeks were flaming. It was adorable, Julie thought.

"That's wonderful!" Alicia exclaimed.

"It is," Julie said. "You know, I've always sort of wondered about you guys."

"Me too," Alicia said, softly.

Julie nodded. "You seemed more like roommates than a married couple."

"Roommates who like each other, but still…" Alicia said.

"It's been like that for a while," Steph agreed. "I don't think either of us meant for it to get that way, but it just happened. Anyway." She smiled again. "There's still a few bumps in the road, but we're fixing things, and it's really great. Like a second honeymoon, at times."

"I am *so* happy for you," Alicia gushed. "That's *amazing*."

Now Julie turned to study Alicia. She seemed…well, yes, so happy for Steph. Did she seem unhappy for herself? She did have not just one but two slices of pizza, instead of a salad like she usually got at their lunches. Was that a sign of greater comfort with herself, or of drowning one's sorrows, or saying 'fuck it'? Julie wanted to ask about her and Ron's marriage…but she also didn't want to touch an electric third rail.

If Alicia wanted to share, this was the obvious opening.

But Alicia just kept grinning at Steph. "It's like a movie," she said. "So romantic! Snowed in, forced to share a bed—and suddenly happily ever after!"

"Yeah, well," Steph said, still blushing as she looked down at her empty plate. "I mean, it's not like we were *un*happy—we were just sort of zombie-ing along in our separate tracks. We needed something to shake us out of our rut."

"A total movie," Alicia said. "One of those Hallmark Christmas movies!"

"Ugh!" Julie said, and laughed, as did Steph.

"All right, that's going maybe a bit overboard," Steph said.

"Is he going to start coming to soup groups?" Alicia asked.

Steph shook her head. "He's still an introvert," she said, and did Julie hear something else behind her words? "So, probably not. But maybe the occasional smaller gathering." She smiled at them. "Like I said, we're still figuring it all out."

"Well, I think it's *wonderful*," Alicia said again, and Julie certainly had to agree.

MATT

MATT DID CALL the clinic about his dad, and told the advice nurse his concerns. The nurse made an appointment, and then called back saying the doctor wanted a full blood panel before they came in, so Matt had to take Gordon down there twice in one week.

When they met with the doctor, she pulled up Gordon's numbers on her laptop. "I do see some minor issues with his kidneys and his liver, but there's nothing too far outside the normal ranges here." She looked over his medication list, asking Gordon a number of questions; he turned to Matt for help in answering most of them.

Then she did a physical examination, proclaiming Gordon to be in very excellent shape for his age.

"But I'm just so tired," Gordon said, grumpily. "Can't you give me something to pep me up a bit?"

"Actually," Matt said, "a friend of mine mentioned some research she'd read about seniors and light and health." He explained to the doctor what Ramona had told him. She listened attentively, but didn't have much to suggest.

"I'll up his dose of the valsartan," she said. "That can help with energy sometimes, and he's on a really low dose—it's certainly safe to increase it a bit and see what happens." She typed as she spoke, then turned to Matt. "Go ahead and give us a call back if you don't see any improvement within a few weeks."

"And about the light?" he asked.

She shrugged. "You could try one of those full-spectrum lamps that people use for seasonal affective disorder."

"Will that help?"

"It couldn't hurt."

Matt went home and ordered a lamp. Getting Gordon to actually use it would be another issue for another day.

ALICIA

SHE MEANT TO spend more time writing out recipes—even though they hadn't actually settled on which exact recipes were going to be included in the cookbook—but then suddenly came one of those "feast" times in a freelancer's feast-or-famine life, when jobs poured in, half of them rush, and none of them on her schedule. Alicia knew darn well that books didn't get written overnight; how in the world did these authors suddenly show up on her doorstep (well, in her email) with completed books that they wanted to publish in two weeks? Were they truly unable to plan ahead sufficiently to even give her some notice?

"Not that I'm complaining," she muttered to herself as she

added yet another new edit to her work calendar. This one was from a beloved longtime client; she'd have to juggle a few other books around to get it done in time, but she would do it. Loyalty was worth plenty, and she knew it would be a fun book.

Fortunately, Ron was still busy with whatever was keeping him so occupied, and so grumpy, in his study for long hours every day. She still suspected it was a new book, even though his last one had not managed to find a publisher. So he hardly noticed that Alicia was holed up over her own computer all the time.

And she did enjoy the money that her work brought in. They could live perfectly comfortably on the combination of Ron's pension and his inheritance, which was well-invested, but Alicia had never felt right about letting a man support her. *I can take care of myself if I need to*, she told herself. *Or if I want to.*

Then her thoughts veered away from what felt like a dangerous direction, and she focused on the new book that had come in. Today was Friday; she'd work on it over the weekend, and probably be able to get it back to her client by mid-next week sometime, if she pushed. It was an off week for soup group; their social calendar was clear.

After spending a few hours getting acquainted with the book and its characters—it turned out to be the start of a new series, so everything was unfamiliar to her—she took a break and went into the kitchen for some lunch. There were some leftovers from last night, a lentil lasagna she'd made, with tons of veggies. Yes, also cheese and noodles, but it was pretty healthy, and super tasty. She heated up a square of it in the microwave, already cringing a little at the thought of Ron's snarkiness about things not heated in the real oven.

Why do I put up with this? she thought, and again tried to push her thoughts away, but they didn't go as easily this time. Instead, she remembered her lunch on Tuesday with Julie and Steph. Steph, who had seemingly been in just as broken a marriage as she was—though the details clearly differed—and yet had somehow, astonishingly, just…fixed it.

How did you even do that?

And do I want to? whispered her traitorous, terrible mind.

Of course she wanted to. She loved Ron. She wouldn't have married him if she hadn't, or stayed with him this long. She'd known that he had a strong personality from the start. It was part of what had attracted her to him: he knew his mind, he had opinions and he wasn't afraid to share them.

And she agreed with so many of those opinions, and respected them all, even the ones she didn't share. He was intellectually exciting, and valued all the same things she did: a life of the mind, a liberal education, being an informed citizen. Good food and good wines.

When had they gone from feeling like a team to feeling like they were in opposition to each other?

She ate her lasagna standing in front of the big picture windows that looked down on the water far below. This wasn't waterfront property per se—there were three levels of lots below them, stepping down the hill, all with houses on them tucked into the trees—but that didn't matter. Seeing the sound made all the difference.

Alicia loved this house, and this view. It had been the first thing she'd noticed when their realtor opened the door. Ron, of course, had claimed his study first off: another room with the same view, off a hallway leading away from the main central space. Ironically, once they'd moved in, he'd set up his desk facing a wall. Did he ever look at the view?

What did he want, anyway?

Yes, she knew what he wanted. He wanted to be—not famous, exactly, but well-regarded. Admired. He wanted his books to be read. He wanted smart people to sit around saying, "That Dr. Ron Alderson: he makes some *very* intelligent points." It didn't even have to be a whole lot of smart people. Just the right ones.

What did he want from Alicia? She thought she knew, once.

He'd wanted companionship, partnership; he'd wanted the company of a smart woman who was also sexy and energetic.

I'm keeping my part of the bargain, she thought.

She finished the lasagna but still felt hungry. Should she heat up another piece? Ugh, too many carbs…especially when the weather was still too miserable to play pickleball. But somehow, she found herself back at the fridge, and before she knew it, a second piece was in the microwave.

What do I want? she asked herself, as the microwave beeped.

She took the plate out and started eating, this time just sitting at the big kitchen island. *I want him to be nice to me. I want him to stop being so unhappy. I want him to find the same kind of joy in his work as I do in mine. I want him to—*

Why are all my thoughts about him? a second voice asked inside her mind.

I want to not walk around my own damn house with my shoulders up around my ears, she thought, feeling filled with sudden anger.

"Okay," she said aloud, getting up and putting her plate in the sink. "Clearly time to go back to work."

She went to her study and tried to lose herself in the new book. It didn't work; the simmering rage kept creeping back in, and several times she realized she'd been staring at the same paragraph for ten minutes, not seeing it.

Whoo, she thought, leaning back in her chair and saving the file. *I don't know where all this came from.*

Or what to do about it.

How *did* you fix a marriage that had lost its way? She and Ron already shared a bed, technically, so she couldn't try Steph's solution.

And do I want to? she asked herself again.

She sat for a long time, not finding an answer. Eventually, she settled on, *If I could get Original Ron back, that would be nice.*

It would be a good start, anyway.

Chapter 5

JULIE

Gavin now got invited to every soup group meeting. He didn't always attend—he hadn't been at the last one, at Ron and Alicia's—but the group considered him one of them now.

Which made Julie very happy.

What made Julie very unhappy was the news that the stupid, dishonest, sneaky, underhanded, probably-illegal-she-didn't-care-what-the-judge-said measure had actually passed. Despite all their efforts getting the word out, the turnout for this special election in the middle of winter had been, as they had feared, very low. It hadn't taken much for the other side to overwhelm the small number of "no" votes.

"I can't believe we lost," she said getting mad all over again, as Gavin drove them up to Matt's house. "I mean, I know why turnout is low in the winter, but it just frustrates the hell out of me. It's not like anyone has to leave the house, we all vote by mail in Washington State!"

"Not to mention turnout is also low for off-year elections, and even more so for special elections," Gavin said. He was at least as unhappy about this as she was, but he was calmer about it. He was always calmer about everything.

This was usually something she loved about him.

"Also," he went on, oh so calmly, "you still do have to leave the house to vote—if only to put your ballot in the mail. Or drive it to the drop box, if you wait till the last minute."

"I think there's something extra fishy going on here," she said. "Who do we ask about getting a recount? Or examining the ballots—was everyone who voted an actual resident? Were their ballots marked properly? Did the county actually send absentee ballots to people who requested them? Did anyone *know* to request absentee ballots?"

Gavin shook his head as he pulled into Matt's driveway, and parked behind Ron and Alicia's car. "I'm not sure questioning the election integrity is the best use of our resources. But we can talk about it with Leslie next week."

"It just makes me so *mad!*" Julie said, as she got out of the car.

"What's wrong?" Alicia asked her, closing their passenger door. Ron circled around behind her and opened the back door, pulling out several bottles of wine in a fancy padded carrier.

"The election!" Julie said. "That stupid measure actually won!"

"Oh, it did? I hadn't heard." Alicia gave her a sympathetic frown. "I'm so sorry, that's terrible."

"Are you going to try to get a measure on the next ballot to repeal it?" Ron asked.

Julie and Gavin looked at each other. "We don't know what we're going to do just yet," Gavin said. "Except drink wine and eat soup, for now."

Alicia laughed, and took Julie's arm. "Come on—he's right, let's drown your sorrows at least for tonight."

Julie tried to force herself to listen to her friends, and to her boyfriend. To be present in this moment, because they were right: there was nothing to be done about any of it on a Sunday night. She allowed herself to be led into Matt's house, and accepted a glass of wine and a seat on the sofa.

But she just wanted to cry, she was so angry. All the work they'd done! It felt so personal—like Sam McLeod was targeting her specifically.

Which, of course, wasn't true, mostly; he had targeted her when he'd had her car towed, and probably when he'd directed his minions to dig up the sidewalk in front of her shop the second time, but his overall effort wasn't about her. She was just someone who had been visibly in his way, however briefly.

Blocking what, though, she still wasn't quite sure. What did he stand to gain in all this?

She shook her head and sipped her wine. These were questions for next week, for down the road. She turned to Lynne, who was sitting on the other end of the sofa, talking to Matt's father, ensconced in his easy chair with a glass of ginger ale by his side.

"I hear you have a new light," Lynne was saying to the old man.

He looked confused, frowning over at her. "A light?"

Lynne nodded. "A full spectrum light, to help with the winter blues. I think it's a great idea. Do you like it?"

"I don't remember any light."

Matt walked into the living room carrying a huge bowl of tortilla chips and a smaller bowl of guacamole. "Yes, Dad, remember? I set it up in your bedroom, and you're supposed to sit in front of it for a little while every morning?"

He still looked confused. Matt set the bowls on the coffee table and said to Lynne, "He thinks it's a computer screen, or the world's most boring TV."

"Oh *that* thing!" Gordon said, shaking his head. "I didn't know what that was for."

Matt gave him a slightly strained smile. "It's for your health. I was telling Lynne about it in the kitchen a few minutes ago; she's a doctor, remember?"

"My doctor at the clinic is also a lady," Gordon said. "I like her."

Julie smiled and took a chip, scooping a good portion of guacamole onto it. Gordon remembered most things that had to do with ladies.

Gavin had followed Matt out from the kitchen; he now squeezed next to Julie on the sofa. "All right?" he whispered into her ear, under the pretext of giving her a little kiss.

"Yes," she told him, smiling at him. "The wine helps, and the company. Especially now." She put her arm around his waist and squeezed.

"Did I hear you guys talking about grow lights?" Gavin asked Matt and Lynne.

Lynne laughed, as Matt said, "I hope not! Full spectrum lights, to use on people, for chasing away the winter blues. Not to help them grow—I hope."

"Same technology, though," Gavin said. "I've got a whole setup of grow lights in my greenhouses, and the seedlings love them."

Alicia and Steph walked in from the kitchen. "I've been wanting to ask you about your greenhouse lights," Steph said to Gavin. "I've got a few plants I want to try in mine that don't work in our climate, and I remember hearing you actually grow poinsettias. I know that temperature is important to them, but it occurred to me that light probably is as well."

Julie sat back and let the conversation wash around her. She was among friends, and loved ones. They all cared about each other, and were helping each other with the issues in their lives, large and small. This bump in the road with the asshole vacation rental guy would be smoothed out.

Perspective is everything, she told herself, as she watched Gavin and Steph geek out over greenhouse technology, while Alicia and Lynne tag-teamed Gordon, working to cheer him up. He was usually such a bright and happy fellow, despite his memory loss. Matt was doing an amazing job with him. It couldn't be easy—especially since Heather had moved out. Julie knew Heather hadn't been Gordon's primary care giver, but she had been helpful, and, at least as far as everyone had thought, supportive.

It just went to show that you never really knew anything about other people's relationships, she thought, yet again.

LYNNE

AT THE END of the evening, after all the hugs and goodbyes, Lynne and Steph got into Lynne's car for the drive home to Deer Harbor.

"I love Matt to the moon and back," Lynne said, "but it is increasingly clear that Heather was the actual cook in that partnership."

Steph chuckled. "Oh, he's just serving things Gordon likes. I know he's capable of more than that."

"Tomato soup and grilled cheese sandwiches, though? Really?" Lynne grinned to show that she wasn't a hundred percent serious. "Please tell me that that one-step-up-from-Campbell's concoction won't be in our illustrious fancy cookbook."

"Oh, I don't know," Steph mused, playing along. "We could do a chapter on Soups Beloved by Young and Old Alike—*Only* Young and Old."

"I don't mean to be unkind," Lynne said, now feeling a little bad for making fun. "I know Gordon enjoys these evenings, and they are good for him. Matt was telling me that his father has been having a rougher time of it lately."

"It can't be easy, for either of them," Steph agreed. "It's a wonderful thing Matt is doing, taking him in like this, devoting so much time and attention to making his life as good as it can be."

"We really do need a better system of caring for our aged in this country," Lynne said.

"We do. I don't know what people without children are supposed to do."

Lynne glanced over at her and nodded. "I don't either, to be honest."

"Unless they have lots of money," Steph said.

"Even then, there's a huge shortage of care workers, and that's only going to get worse as the population continues to age."

"Ugh."

They drove along in silence for a while, each lost in their own thoughts.

On their drive to soup group earlier this evening, Lynne had asked Steph how she was doing, and, surprisingly, the question had elicited more detail than they usually shared with each other, with Steph telling Lynne about work she and David had been doing on their marriage. "I told Julie and Alicia about all this at lunch last week, and then I realized I hadn't even talked to you about it," Steph had said.

"Well, that's all right," Lynne had said. "You see them more often than you see me." *And they're closer to your age,* she added silently.

"Yeah, but we're next-door neighbors."

Lynne had shrugged. "And I'm in the clinic half the time, and you're busy too; it's not like we're popping over for coffee like people who live in a sitcom."

"Yes, I know..."

"I'm happy for you, though," Lynne had told her. "You both deserve happiness, it seems to me, though of course I don't know David all that well." He did always seem to be working; Steph was the social one.

Now, Steph was clearly back to thinking about it, because she broke their silence to say, "Did it never seem weird to you, to become friends with me while barely knowing my husband?"

Lynne thought about it. "Not really. People move to the islands for lots of reasons. Some of those reasons are because they want to get away from other people, to *not* make new friends, get chummy with the neighbors, all that. I try to respect everyone's needs and wants, and meet them where they are."

Steph smiled. "I knew there was a reason I liked you."

"Well, I like you too. I was glad when you and David bought that house, and gladder still when you decided to make the move up here full-time."

"Until you learned we were about to embark on a noisy, messy remodel!"

"Oh, that didn't bother me."

In her purse, her phone rang. "Do you want me to see who that is?" Steph asked.

"Sure."

She rummaged around and found the phone. "It's your son. Should I answer it? I can tell him you're driving and you'll call him back in a few minutes."

"Go ahead and put it on speaker, let's see what he wants."

"Hey Mom?" came Ethan's voice, a moment later.

"Hi Ethan," Lynne said. "I'm in the car with Steph, so if you have secrets to tell, they'll have to wait."

He laughed. "No secrets! Unless you want to hide the fact that I'd like to come up and see you in a few weeks, if you're around."

"I'm always around, you know that. When were you thinking of coming?"

"The weekend of the first? Marie's got a big thing at work all weekend—they're part of a festival for something or other, I don't remember what, and I thought that would be a good time for me to get out of her hair."

"Well, that was my next question," Lynne said. "So, no Marie, just you." She glanced at Steph, who was trying to whisper something. "What is it?" she asked.

"That weekend is the next soup group," Steph said. "The one you're hosting."

"Oh, I can find another time," Ethan said, but Lynne shook her head.

"No, come then, that would be perfect! I think you know everyone in the group, and you can help me with things."

"Are you sure?"

"Entirely sure. It will be wonderful to see you."

"Okay, sounds good! I'll let you go for now, before you drive through a dead zone and hang up on me."

Lynne chuckled. "Let me know when you've got your ferries."

"Will do."

He hung up, and Steph slipped the phone back into Lynne's purse. "It will be nice to see him," Lynne said, and then added, "Ugh, but I have to excavate Ethan's bedroom."

"From what?"

Oh, right. "Well, speaking of things we next-door neighbors who are dear friends keep neglecting to tell each other…"

Steph was at least as excited about the solo gallery show as Julie and her daughters had been. "I can't believe you've been sitting on this news!" she exclaimed. "Or that Kate didn't tell me!"

"Probably Kate has changed her mind and decided not to have the show after all, and has just been trying to figure out how to tell me," Lynne said, so deadpan that Steph turned to glare at her before laughing.

"More likely she thought you'd already told me," Steph said.

"I should have, but I just didn't think about it," Lynne said. "To be honest, most of my time has been spent agonizing over what to show, and trying to decide whether I need to make a dozen new pieces."

"Do you want me to come over and look at what you've got?"

Lynne started to say no, because Julie had already offered to come do that, but then realized that two sets of eyes would be twice as good as one—and might be just what she needed. "Yes, actually, that would be great. I've been too much in my own head about it, and I can't even see the work anymore. I pulled everything out and draped it all over the place…which is how Ethan's room got into such a state."

"I'll be happy to help. I love looking at your work."

"And now we have a deadline—two weeks."

"I probably shouldn't say this," Steph said, "because I know having a deadline is very motivating, but Ethan can sleep at our house anytime you need."

Lynne smiled. "Thank you, but you're right: knowing I have to figure this out soon will be helpful. Besides, I want my boy with me—and he'll want to be in his own space."

"That makes sense. But the offer stands, for now or anytime you need."

"Thank you."

Steph nodded. "When do you want me to come over? Are you around tomorrow, or are you filling in at the clinic?"

"So far I'm free tomorrow, but I often don't hear till the morning. I can let you know when I know—usually by nine, if someone is calling in sick."

"Sounds good. I'll be home."

"I'll call Julie too—she also wants to help me choose the pieces. Maybe it'll distract her from being so annoyed about the election."

"Good idea. Poor Julie."

They had passed the West Sound Harbor by now and were wending their way down Deer Harbor Road, and soon, Lynne pulled into Steph's driveway. As usual, she waited till her friend had gotten inside to pull out and park in front of her own house.

Once inside, Lynne went into Ethan's room and stood looking at all her tapestries, drapings, decorative cloths, and blankets. *Why am I so frightened of this?* she wondered. *What is art for, if not to share with the world?*

Or, whatever small sliver of the world would visit a gallery on tiny, remote Orcas Island during a few weeks in May.

Well, at least this is forcing me to think about my work, she told herself. *Do I want to be an artist? I know how to be a doctor. I don't know how to do…the rest of this.*

Was it too late to become someone different?

I've always been a person who does fiber art, she corrected herself. *I was a doctor who did art on the side. The only difference here is I could be an artist who does doctoring on the side.*

Was it too late to expand this part of herself that had always been a sideline? To begin to set down her Dr. Lynne Daniels identity and embrace Lynne Daniels, Fiber Artist?

There was only one way to find out.

STEPH

THE HALL LIGHT was on when she got home, but the living room was dark. She peered in there anyway; the fire wasn't lit, and David wasn't there.

Pushing aside her disappointment—they hadn't actually arranged that they'd end the evening in there together, it was just something they'd been doing lately, and she hadn't realized how much she'd been looking forward to it until it suddenly didn't happen—she went to look for him. Their bedroom was empty; was he in his office? At this time of night?

She found him in there, at his desk reading. At least he'd left the door open.

"Hey," she said, tapping lightly on the doorframe, not wanting to startle him.

He set something on the desk and turned to her. "Hey, you're home. How was it?"

"Fine—I mean, fun, good." She smiled at him, continuing to stuff her small sadness as she stepped into the room. "What are you reading?"

He gathered together a scattering of materials on his desk and stacked them on top of the thing he'd set down. "Oh, just some market newsletters that have been piling up up. I didn't realize how late it had gotten."

Now she felt a huge flood of relief—he'd just lost track of time, not forgotten their new rhythms! Or changed his mind about them. "Shall we go sit by a fire in the living room for a bit?"

He frowned. "Actually, I'm kind of tired. Would it be all right if we just went to bed?"

"Of course," she said.

"I'll be in in a few minutes."

"Sure." She turned to go, her eye catching on his last name, printed on the corner of a large envelope that stuck out under the pile he'd just made—where the return address would go, if it were a piece of mail. Before she could ask him about it, he straightened the pile and gave her a strained smile.

She went and brushed her teeth. He followed her into their room a minute later.

In bed, she snuggled against him, breathing in his scent, loving it as much as she'd loved it from the first time they'd slept together—no, even before that, from when they'd first kissed. He fell asleep quickly. It took her a bit longer.

IN THE MORNING, Steph made them both breakfast—Spanish omelets alongside homemade English muffins with a side of fruit in Greek yogurt, a combination that always privately amused her. *International breakfast*, she thought. Now all she needed to do was find one of those tins of awful flavored instant coffees from the eighties, the supposedly fancy "international" stuff.

But nobody would get the joke except her.

Today was one of David's days to work in his office in town. Maybe it would do him good to get out of the house; he seemed distracted and weary, as if he hadn't slept well, though he professed to feel fine.

"Well, have a good day," she said as he got up and took his dishes to the sink.

"Thanks, you too."

She got up with her own plate and coffee mug. "I'm thinking salmon for dinner, with wild rice and mushrooms," she told him, hoping for some spark of enthusiasm, or even interest.

"Sounds good."

She pulled him in for a hug, then drew back, looking up at him. "Are you sure you're okay? You seem…not quite right."

"I'm fine." He gave her a half-smile. "Just still tired, I guess."

"All right." She tilted her face up for a kiss, which he gave her. "Don't work too hard today."

"I won't."

After she cleaned up the dishes, she sat down at the kitchen island with a second cup of coffee and thought for a while. She respected David's privacy and his agency, so she was loath to snoop, but…he had hidden something on his desk from her, hadn't he? An envelope, a big one. He'd shoved it under a pile of innocuous things as she walked into the room.

What was in it?

And why was he keeping it from her?

She sipped her coffee and sighed. Eventually, she came to a decision: something wasn't right, and she loved him; she would not be able to help him if she didn't understand what was going on.

In his study, she worried that he'd have stashed the envelope away in a locked drawer or even taken it to his office in town this morning, but it was right where he'd tucked it. Somehow, this made her feel even worse: he trusted that she wouldn't go looking through his things, that whatever he left on his desk would remain private.

Her guilt wasn't bad enough to keep her from pulling it out, though.

It was a thick nine-by-twelve-inch mailer from Palmer Investments, sent to him at their P.O. box, with a return address in Atherton, California. His parents' company? She knew David's father was in finance, though she didn't know many details.

The envelope had been carefully slit open. Steph hesitated only a moment before reaching in and pulling out the contents.

Most of what she found inside were several glossy, expensively produced quarterly and annual reports of the kind that usually littered David's desk, plus a few "for internal review only" spreadsheets, all to do with Palmer Investments. On top of the stack, affixed with a silver binder clip, was a handwritten note on heavy cream-colored stationery with KATHRYN PALMER embossed across the top. The writing was the elegant cursive of an older woman, one who had clearly received penmanship awards in elementary school.

Dear David,

Please find attached the latest relevant materials and your dividend check. Your father and I are concerned that the bank may soon declare the previous checks mailed to you stale; please ensure that you deposit this one, and the others, in a timely fashion.

We remain concerned as well at your continued noncommunication. It is imperative that you respond to our inquiries; time is running short.

Sincerely,

Mother

Steph stood holding the note, staring at it, struggling to process—well, all of it. His *mother* had written him, obviously more than once, and he hadn't told her about it? No wonder he was upset. But why keep it a secret?

When had this started?

And what was this about checks? She'd found no check in the envelope, though she set the note down and looked through the reports again to be sure.

What was he doing with dividend checks—from his parents' company? Not cashing them, obviously. Was he just destroying them? Steph knew he didn't care much about money. Not nearly as much as his parents did: his parents who had tried so hard to control him that he'd broken free of their influence as soon as he had been able to, in his early twenties.

What did they want from him now? *Time is running short.* Time for what?

In her pocket, her phone buzzed with a text, startling her badly. She scrambled to pull it out, guiltily convinced it was David, asking her what she was doing nosing around in his private office.

But it was Lynne. *I'm free today if you want to come tell me how awful my textiles are! Julie's coming too, she'll be here around eleven.*

Steph took a deep breath, forced her mental voice into "cheerful" mode, and texted back.

There is no universe in which I am available to tell you lies about how awful your art is, but I'd be happy to come help you choose the best pieces for your show!

Lynne answered a minute later: *It's a deal!*

Steph tucked her phone away. Eleven was in about an hour; she still had some time.

She sank into David's office chair, staring at his mother's note for another few minutes. Then she put everything back in the envelope, hoping it was in the order she'd found it in, and replaced it under the stack of unrelated market reports.

Before she could talk herself out of it, she opened all his desk drawers and looked through them. But she didn't find any other Palmer Investments materials, and certainly no uncashed checks. He had a small filing cabinet in here as well; also nothing.

I don't know what to do.

The obvious thing would be to confront David about it. Ask him what his parents wanted and why he'd kept this from her. But…he'd started seeming fragile again lately, after such dramatic improvement; it might be more prudent to gather more information, more obliquely. Maybe it was time to call his therapist, who of course could not reveal private patient information, but who had been quite helpful over the years in suggesting strategies to Steph for opening up productive lines of communication between her and David, and in warning her off topics that would be likely to send him into a depressive spiral.

It was a big deal, though, calling the therapist; something she did not undertake lightly. She really wished she could talk to a friend about this, but…well, she also really did want to respect David's privacy. She always had. This, however, was a new wrinkle. She had never before known him to keep issues from her—certainly not anything this large. This was different, and it was alarming. She should not be expected to navigate this alone.

Running this by a girlfriend would be the safest, gentlest first step.

Who should she talk to? Lynne was caught up in her excitement and anxiety about her show; Alicia was caught up in the emotional whirlwind that was Ron. Maybe Julie? Julie was sensible and sensitive, warm and caring. Yes, Julie would be a good choice.

Steph took one last look around David's study, making sure everything was as it had been before turning off the lights and closing the door behind her.

JULIE, LYNNE, AND Steph crowded together in Ethan's bedroom/Lynne's studio. It looked like a scene from the Arabian Nights. "Seriously," Steph said, picking up one end of a long, narrow piece of cloth that had an intricately worked scene picked out in tiny, precise stitches. "This is astonishing—I would buy this to put over our mantelpiece."

"My god, yes," Julie agreed. "I've never seen anything quite like it." She picked up the other end and studied it closely, as Lynne rocked from foot to foot, clearly forcing herself not to push the compliments away. "Is this Crow Valley?"

"Yes!" Lynne gave them both a shy smile, which seemed so odd on her. The woman was a *doctor*, for crying out loud—one who had gotten her medical degree at a time when few women were doing so. She always seemed so relaxed and self-confident. Steph hadn't realized how much anxiety and insecurity she brought to her creative work. "I keep seeing that scene as I drive by, and I always thought it looked like a painting. Well, I don't paint, but I thought…"

"You thought right," Julie said. "I wish I had a wall space big enough—I'd fight Steph for the right to buy it."

"Bidding war!" Steph said, forcing herself to laugh.

Lynne looked like she wanted to melt through the floor. Which was ridiculous.

"Lynne, I'm serious," Steph told her. "This is gorgeous, and amazing. Unbelievably complex and intricate." This, at least, she did not have to fake: she, like Julie, had never seen anything like it. "You should put this in the show for sure, but I'm also serious about this: do not list it for sale. I want to buy it."

"I will give it to you—" Lynne started, but Steph interrupted her.

"Nope. Don't even. In fact, I'm not going to ask you to put a price on it—we're going to get Kate to do it."

Lynne looked even more mortified than before, which was quite an accomplishment. "At least tell her you're buying it, so she can price it accordingly! I can't charge you what I'd charge a perfect stranger."

Steph was still shaking her head, as was Julie. "Nope again," Steph said. "Kate is going to price all your pieces, and after she does that, we'll tell her that this one is not for sale, and that's the end of that." She set the piece aside, lovingly, and started looking at all the other objects of incredible beauty. There was not an inch of the room that wasn't draped in something amazing.

Julie was now holding a smaller, more brightly colored abstract piece from a pile on a chair under the window. "Now *this* is something I'd have room for…"

"I'll—" Lynne started, but both Julie and Steph interrupted her.

"You're not giving away anything!" They looked at each other and laughed. "Jinx," Julie said.

"You're overruled," Steph told Lynne. "What's this pile over here?" She made her way to the far corner of the room, beside the closet.

"Oh, just second-tier stuff…"

Steph started looking through it. It was all, of course, just as gorgeous as the rest.

"Wow," Julie said, holding up another smallish piece—a depiction of a koi pond that could have been a photograph, except better. "You just sit here in your chair and do all this in the evenings? And never show it to anyone?"

"That piece didn't really come out like I'd hoped…"

Steph laughed. "Oh, boy, do we have work to do here."

It took several hours, but Steph and Julie were able to overcome at least a little bit of Lynne's almost pathological fear of recognizing her own talent and get her to help in choosing representative work. It was also very helpful in distracting Steph from this morning's discovery, and her dilemma. "Every single piece in this room is more than good enough to go into a show," Steph told Lynne, "but this is a good cross-section of the different kinds of things that you do, and yet they all work together. Kate will want to weigh in, but that's all right: this is probably too many pieces. She can winnow it down."

"Actually, that's a good idea, giving her too much," Julie said. "Put the concept of a second show in her mind…maybe we should add a few pieces."

"Ooh, I like how you think," Steph said, diving back into the pile of things that hadn't made the final cut.

"I don't know how to thank you both," Lynne said, nearly another hour later. "I'm still having a hard time believing these are show-worthy, but you're starting to wear me down. Just a little."

"Good." Steph smiled. "You can thank me by coming over for lunch later this week. You too, if you can," she added, to Julie.

"That sounds great," Julie said. "Which day?"

"I'm not sure yet—I have some ingredients to find. I can let you know."

"Perfect," Julie said. "Anything else we can help you with here today?"

Lynne laughed. "Oh gosh. I think you've both done more than enough."

"I'll head back to town then," Julie said. "Let me know about lunch."

"Will do."

"I'll walk you out," Steph told Julie, as Lynne began folding the unchosen pieces.

At Julie's car, Steph said, "I'd love to run something by you, if you have time to get together for coffee or a drink soon."

"Of course," Julie said, looking at Steph with concern. "Is everything all right?"

"I don't know," Steph admitted. "Sorry to be mysterious, but I could use a little more time to think about it myself first."

"Call me," Julie said, opening her car door. "But I will call you if I don't hear from you in the next day or two."

Steph smiled at her gratefully. "I'll call, I promise."

Back inside, Lynne gave Steph a mock-frown. "So, about this lunch."

"Yes?"

"I am always thrilled to eat anything you cook, but I think you're confused about how gratitude works. If anything, I should be making *you* lunch. You've just spent half your day here helping me out."

Steph laughed. "But I actually do need a favor, and you're the perfect person to help me. I'm working on a new take on savory pies, and I need to know if anything I've tried is working or not."

"Sounds intriguing. What does David think of them?"

With a suppressed sigh, Steph said, "David loves everything I cook, so he's no help. Please? Any time later this week works for me."

"Most days should work for me too—with the usual caveats about being on call."

"Understood. I'll let you know when I've got what I need."

Lynne gave her friend a grateful smile. "Yes. And thank you again for your help and support today. Particularly the support."

Steph held her gaze. "It was truly my pleasure—and I know Julie loved it too."

Lynne nodded, and pulled Steph into a strong hug. "Talk to you soon."

"Absolutely."

Steph walked slowly down the path between their houses, thinking about creativity, and self-esteem, and the way so many women hid what was best and brightest about themselves in… well, in a back bedroom.

JULIE

WHEN SHE GOT back to town, Julie swung by the post office to pick up her mail. In among the usual bills and catalogues, she found an official-looking notice from the County of San Juan.

Odd, she thought, tearing the envelope open right in the post office lobby.

Inside was a one-page letter, purportedly from the Eastsound Historical Character and Beautification Commission, which could not possibly exist yet; it had been voted into existence barely a week ago.

It was a form letter, with her name and the name of her store handwritten at the top.

Dear Business Owner,

In the interest of Preserving and Beautifying Eastsound's Historical Character, this Commission will be conducting an in-depth zoning survey of all properties on Main Street, North Beach Road, and Prune Alley. It has come to the attention of the Commission that many business properties may include inappropriate storage, manufacturing, or residential facilities.

The Eastsound Downtown Business District is zoned for retail activities only. Retail activities include the sale of merchandise, food, and services. All other uses are not allowed.

This letter serves as your notice that Commission inspectors will be visiting every Eastsound place of business over the next six (6) weeks. Please make your entire premises available to the inspection team when they arrive to ensure an efficient inspection process.

Thank you for your cooperation. Together, we will Preserve and

Beautify Historical Eastsound!

The letter was signed with a photocopy of an illegible scrawl.

What fresh hell is this? Julie thought, standing at the table by the post office's front window. She briefly wondered if one of her friends was playing an elaborate prank on her, but she didn't know anyone who would be so mean. No, this had to be real—even if it wasn't legal or legitimate.

She read the letter again, her blood pressure rising with every word. Resisting the urge to crumple it up and hurl it at the post office's trash bin, she instead pulled out her phone and called Leslie Magnas.

"Where can I find Sam McLeod? I mean in person."

Leslie chuckled. "Well, hello to you too, Julie."

"Sorry. Hi. Where can I find Sam McLeod?"

"He doesn't have a dedicated office here that I know of, but Rina at Sunset Properties usually lets him use a desk when he's on the island."

"Great. Thanks."

"Of course, he's in Seattle a lot of the time—"

"I'll find him." She hung up before Leslie had finished her sentence and stomped out of the post office, walking down North Beach Road to the real estate office Leslie had mentioned.

The bell over the door jangled as she opened it, and a young blond woman looked up from a desk. "Can I help you?"

"I'm looking for Sam McLeod."

"He doesn't work—"

"I *know*," Julie interrupted, "but I'm told he uses a desk here when he's on island." She scanned the large room; mostly empty desks, with one realtor talking on the phone near a back window. "Is he here?"

"He's not right now," the woman said. "He left about an hour ago."

Just my luck! "Where did he go, do you know?"

The woman hesitated, then must have seen something in Julie's face that struck her sympathy. "Well, I can't say for sure, but he often goes over to the Lower for a beer or two."

"Really?" Julie was incredulous. Fancy city-slicker Sam McLeod, slumming it with the locals? She couldn't see it.

"He, ah, he likes the sports, I think," said the young woman with a shrug.

"Well, good for him. Thanks." Julie turned back to the door, pausing with her hand on the handle. "Don't warn him I'm coming."

The young woman gave her a knowing nod.

At the Lower Tavern, she paused just inside the door to let her eyes adjust to the dim light. It was mid-afternoon, but at least half the tables and most of the barstools were occupied. One of the big-screen TVs was showing a basketball game; another showed hockey.

Aha, there he was: sitting at the first booth beside the bar with a pint glass of beer in front of him. Across from him was another man, slightly younger, bearded, and dressed like an islander in stained Carhartt's, an oversized hoodie, and a well-worn baseball cap. The local had his own pint glass; a half-empty pitcher sat between them. They seemed deep in conversation.

As she strode across the room toward the men, she realized that McLeod himself was in islander-workman drag as well: faded jeans, plaid flannel shirt, and work boots. Except his boots were pristine, and she could see the crease pressed into his jeans from here. Probably his shirt still had the tag on it somewhere.

She came to a stop at the edge of their table, leaning over it. McLeod paused what he was saying and looked up at her with a bland smile, obviously assuming she was a server. She waved the letter under his nose and said, "What the hell is this?"

Across from Sam, the other man reared back in surprise, but McLeod just continued looking up at her mildly. "Ms. Pessel. It's lovely to see you again too."

"I mean it, McLeod: this can't possibly be legal or even real. Are you looking to be sued for harassment?"

He blinked innocently. "Excuse me?"

She shook the letter again. "Businesses not being zoned for residential? That's bullshit and you know it. Everything about my house and shop is entirely legitimate and above-board—I made sure of it when I bought the business. I do not appreciate being singled out like this just because I objected to your men trying to slap *parking meters* in front of my store."

Now his eyes narrowed slightly. "Ms. Pessel, I can assure you, you are not being singled out in any way. Every single business owner in the Eastsound Business District has received one of these exact same letters. Just as every single business owner will be expected to comply with the regulations when the commission has them all squared away."

"The *new* regulations, you mean; and how did you sneak those through, anyway? For that matter, who even sent this letter? You can't possibly have any commissioners yet—I'm not even sure the election results have been certified."

"Not that it's any business of yours, but the working group has been eager to get going. They drafted this letter and I approved it."

"The 'working group'? Who are they?"

Sam picked up his pint glass and took a slow, deliberate sip before setting the glass carefully on the table once more. He leaned back and folded his arms across his chest. "My apologies. I didn't realize you'd been appointed to the county council. I'll be sure and get your approval before I authorize any more actions of duly elected commissions, Councilor Pessel." He gave her a mocking smile: *Your move.*

Julie exhaled through her nose, fighting the urge to scream. Across from Sam, the other man watched them both with avid (or was it aghast?) interest. "Fine," Julie said at last. "I'll find out who this 'working group' is—because they are certainly not *duly elected commissioners*—and we'll get to the bottom of this." *And*

I will dig up my purchase records for the house and shop, she prom-ised herself. "You will not get away with this." She turned on her heel, preparing to storm back out of the tavern, but it had gotten much more crowded in the last few minutes; there was no clear path to the door.

"Always a pleasure, Councilor Pessel," Sam said to her back. "You take care now."

Julie fumed her way through the crowd and out the door. As she stomped up the street toward her house, her phone buzzed in her pocket.

She pulled it out to find a text from Leslie: *I think I've been more than patient enough, Pessel. Are you going to tell me what's going on, or do I have to come down there and shake it out of you?*

Julie exhaled a laugh as she started typing back to Leslie, then changed her mind and called her. "Are you sitting down?"

"Always. Give it to me straight: do we need to take out a hit on McLeod?"

"Oh, don't tempt me. Don't *even* tempt me."

Chapter 6

JULIE

Steph called her the next afternoon to follow up on their coffee-or-drink get-together.

"Drink, definitely," Julie said. "I have something to run by you as well that will absolutely require alcohol. Want to meet at the Barnacle?"

After a hesitation, Steph said, "I love the Barnacle but it's a little...less private than I'd like. Could I just come to your house—your shop isn't open today, is it?"

"No, I'm still on Fridays through Sundays till March first. You're more than welcome to come here."

"I'll even bring the wine."

"No need for that!" Julie assured her.

"And snacks," Steph added.

Julie shook her head, smiling. "I suppose there's no stopping you, is there?"

"Nope, so you might as well not fight it."

Thirty minutes later, they sat at Julie's kitchen table, a bottle of Pinot Noir between them, next to a platter of medjool dates stuffed with mascarpone cheese and rolled in chopped pistachios, which were so delicious it was hard to concentrate.

Except that what Steph was telling her was riveting.

"Wow," Julie said, leaning back and sipping her wine. "So, you've never even *met* his parents, and now suddenly they're sending him demanding letters and business documents—and money? And he's not mentioning any of this to you?"

Steph nodded sadly. "We've never kept secrets from each other. Even at the worst of his depression, when he could barely talk, he would at least try to tell me what was going on—as best he could. But now he's just saying he's fine. Or tired." She shook her head and pushed her wine glass back and forth absently on the table. "After we'd made such progress reconnecting."

"I know. I was so happy for you."

"So was I." Steph sighed. "Stupid me."

"You are *not* stupid," Julie said forcefully.

"Naïve maybe." Before Julie could reassure her again, Steph asked, "So should I confront him about this? Just tell him what I found and ask him what's going on?"

Julie thought about it a minute. "You realize you're asking marital advice from a divorced woman, right?"

"Your divorce is ancient history, and you've told me it was amicable and that you're friendly with your ex. *And*, you're in a marvelous new relationship that's already weathered a challenge and only got stronger for it."

Julie smiled. "Well, I suppose that's all true. But still." She picked up a date and bit into it, buying a bit more time to think while she chewed. "Ordinarily, I would say absolutely. Even if you didn't have a history of full disclosure and honesty, I think openness is always the best option in any relationship."

"But?"

"Yeah. But." She took a breath. "The trouble with this particular issue is—well, it's his parents. The people who hurt him so badly in the first place. I know we don't know what causes depression, but from what you've told me, they absolutely did him no favors growing up—at the very least, they made everything a whole lot worse for him." She ate the second half of the date before going on. "I mean, going full-on no contact in his early twenties—and holding that line for nearly thirty years—this is no small thing. This isn't some little adolescent rebellion or a few bruised feelings."

"I consider them his first abusers," Steph said quietly. "His original bullies."

"It certainly sounds like it." Julie washed her latest date down with another sip of wine. "So I would worry about you triggering something if you tried to press him about this right now."

"Not to mention the fact that I only found out about it by snooping in his office," Steph said. "Which, like I said, I've never done before."

"I don't consider that such a trespass," Julie said. "As you also said, he's never kept things from you before. I'd say you're at least even there."

Steph shook her head. "No, I'm not happy with what I did. I just didn't know what else to do."

"Let's leave that aside for now." Julie studied her friend. Steph was usually so full of life, of energy. Julie was not sure she'd ever seen her this downtrodden. "I think, if I were you, I would do what I could to ease him out of the corner he's in. Let him know he's safe with you, he's loved. Share as much of *your* life with him as possible—tell him what you do with your days, what you watched on TV, your hopes and dreams. Ask him about his days, but don't get weird about it. Just encourage him to open up about anything—especially low-stakes stuff." She watched Steph as she spoke. "Is any of this making sense?"

"Yeah, it is," she said slowly. "So his parents have backed him into this corner, and maybe I can coax him out?"

Julie shrugged. "Maybe. I think it's worth a try, at least. It's how you guys got together in the first place, right? Your, what, cheerful, patient persistence?"

Steph smiled. "Pretty much."

"That worked, when the break with his parents was still fresh for him. Show him that's still the dynamic between you two. Now, if nothing changes, I'd say you should ask more pointed questions. But I don't see any harm in trying a gentler approach at first."

Steph was slowly nodding. Then she frowned. "I just can't help wondering about the timing of it all…if any of this has to do with our, um, refreshing of things between us."

Julie leveled a look at her. "You mean his mom somehow spidey-sensed that you guys were getting it on again, and decided to, what, rope him back into her toxic web?"

Steph snorted. "Well, when you put it like that, it does sound kind of silly." She pushed her wine glass back and forth between her fingers again, then seemed to realize what she was doing; she took a sip, then set the glass farther away from herself. "You're right. I'm trying to make this thing about me when it obviously isn't."

"Except for the part where it's about your marriage," Julie said. "But I think, given the decades of love and trust and happiness you have under your belts, you have time to try the approach that's worked before. If this whole thing with his parents is as recent as it seems, he's likely frozen, panicking—it's probably shoved him back into his childhood trauma. But he's not a helpless child now, at their mercy; he's an adult, married to a smart and compassionate woman who supports him one hundred percent, and who always has. Once his panic eases, he may well open up to you on his own. Then you can face whatever it is together."

"I like that," Steph said, nodding again. "It makes a lot of sense. Even though it also sort of feels like a cowardly approach."

"Cowardly?"

"You know. 'Oh, confrontation is so scary; why don't I just pretend like nothing's wrong for a while and see if things get better on their own.'"

Julie laughed. "Well, despite what I'm about to tell you, I don't always think direct confrontation is the best way to get things accomplished."

"Okay, now I'm intrigued." Steph was perking up. Julie was glad to see it.

She related her encounter with Sam McLeod, and found herself even able to laugh about it. Well, a little. "I mean, where does he get off, having his 'working group' sending official letters to every Eastsound business owner? What's the big hurry here, anyway?"

"It does seem weird," Steph agreed. "But I love the image of you marching in there and throwing his letter in his face, and telling him what-for."

"And then having to 'excuse me, pardon me' my way out of there when I was done," Julie said, laughing.

"Who was the other guy, the one with him?"

Juile shrugged. "No idea. He never said a word."

"He looked local, though?"

"He did. Maybe a contractor or something."

Steph nodded, and even reached out to take one of the dates. "I suppose local contractors would stand to do really well if a whole bunch of new zoning regulations came into being."

"Maybe, but I never had the impression that they were hurting for work before now. It's impossible to get anyone to do a minor home repair job these days—they're all busy building McMansions for wealthy off-islanders."

"Including vacation rental developers," Steph added.

"Hmm." They looked at each other for a minute, considering this. "I still don't see the angle though," Julie added. "Why does a wealthy off-island vacation rental developer want to remake Eastsound? I mean, 'beautification'? The town is already perfectly beautiful just as it is. It's authentic, and quaint; visitors flock to it by the thousands every year. What's he trying to do—make it like any other cookie-cutter tourist town the world over?"

"Ugh. We're not *Carmel*," Steph said.

"Exactly!"

STEPH

ON FRIDAY, LYNNE and Steph sat at Steph's kitchen island—Julie, alas, was working in her shop and had to miss the tasting. Steph had four different pies set before them, with a few slices missing from each one, because though David was no help with the choosing, that didn't mean he didn't get to eat them. She'd taken Julie's advice to heart and had been warm and chatty and nonconfrontational with David. He'd seemed more relaxed for the last few days; they'd even cuddled before the fire last night after dinner.

Now Steph cut four more small slices and dished them onto eight plates—with eight clean forks. She knew Lynne was watching her with amusement, but, well, you couldn't mix up the flavors, could you? That would negate the whole experiment.

"Okay, I'm not going to tell you what's in each one until you taste it."

"Sounds good."

"And after you've tasted them all, I want you to tell me which one you like best, and why, if you know."

"I guess you *are* making me work for this," Lynne said with a smile. "Should I be making tasting notes?"

Steph laughed. "No, not unless you want to."

"I think I can wing it." Lynne picked up her first fork and took a bite of her first slice.

Steph did the same, so the flavors would be fresh on her palate while Lynne talked about them.

"Hmm, interesting," Lynne said, chewing slowly and looking thoughtful. "I can't quite identify all the flavors, but I like the meat—it's both hearty and tender. Is it lamb?"

Steph nodded. "Yep."

"Wonderful. And in some kind of Middle Eastern spice, but not one I'm familiar with. It works; the sweetness really helps."

"Thanks." Steph chewed as well, following along.

"Are these carrots?"

"Sweet potatoes," Steph said. "And it's actually mostly a north African spice, not Middle Eastern, but you're close."

Lynne nodded. "I want more of it, but I feel like I should try a bite of each one first, right?"

"I don't think it matters. As long as you're not full before we get to the end."

Lynne picked up her glass of water and took a sip, swishing it around in her mouth before swallowing.

"Do you want something else to cleanse your palate with?" Steph asked, already halfway off of her stool to see what she had in the fridge.

"No, no, this is perfect." She grabbed a clean fork and aimed it at her second slice, taking a generous bite. "Mmm, this is rich. Very nice." She chewed, again thinking. "Chicken, obviously, but this is nothing like a traditional chicken pot pie. Definitely butter, and I love the garlic and all the herbs. What are the vegetables?"

"Jerusalem artichokes, in a sauce of pureed cooked boy choy and baby kale, mostly. And, you know, other stuff."

"Of course." Lynne took another small bite. "How do you come up with these ideas?"

"I don't know—I just like to eat, and I enjoy thinking about what flavors and textures might be good together. But as I said, I don't always know what's going to work. Not everyone likes weird experimental food."

"I do, lucky me." Lynne put her fork down with obvious reluctance and took another cleaning sip of water before picking up her third clean fork. "Ooh, scallops," she said, before even putting it in her mouth.

"Mm-hmm," Steph said, watching her friend take the bite.

Lynne's eyes widened. "Oh, that's nice. I didn't expect the spice—that's got some heat to it."

"Is it too much?"

"Not for me it isn't. But everyone's different." She rolled the bite around on her tongue. "Again, good use of sweetness, though completely different from the lamb pie. This balances the spice nicely; there's almost a vinegar note too."

"Yes! Rice wine vinegar, and a sweet chili sauce I made and put away last summer."

Lynne swallowed, looking like she was concentrating. "This isn't pumpkin, or sweet potato."

"Kabocha squash," Steph told her. "Roasted first, with some ginger dressing—or would you rather I let you guess?"

Lynne shrugged. "I'm never going to guess everything you come up with—I don't know if I would even recognize that squash if I saw one." She took another bite. "I do taste the ginger, yes. But it's subtle, under the chili sauce. It works."

"Do you have a favorite yet?" Steph couldn't help asking.

"I love them all! But so far, I think the—no, wait, I mean the—no, sorry, I don't. Each time I try to name one of them, I remember the others."

Steph looked pointedly at the fourth slice in front of Lynne.

"You're a cruel woman," Lynne said, and sighed. "Okay: onward."

Steph watched her carefully. The fourth pie was…well, to be fair, just as with Lynne, they were all her favorites, but this one was particularly interesting to her. And it went along with the theme she was trying to build better than the others…

"*Wow*," Lynne said, closing her eyes in bliss. "I mean, just, wow."

"You like it?"

"It's amazing. What *is* this? I can't identify a thing."

Steph beamed at her. "Sure you can. What's the protein?"

"It's not—is this *tofu*?"

"It is. Marinated and roasted."

"It's *so* good." She took a second bite. "And what's the squash, more kachoba?"

"Kabocha, and no; it's actually unripe butternut squash."

Lynne laughed. "Where do you even *find* half these things?"

"Oh, here and there. The co-op. Online. My greenhouses. You know."

"And the coconut milk really brings it all together. I like the hint of lemon."

Steph gave her a satisfied smile. "There's no lemon in this pie."

"So what am I tasting?"

"Lemongrass! I've totally fallen in love with lemongrass, but it's hard to get hold of here. I want to start growing it—it's why I was talking to Gavin about his greenhouses."

"Wow. This is definitely my favorite pie." Lynne took a third bite, bigger than her first two. "I mean, the others were all incredible, but this one—I've never tasted anything like it. And I don't want to stop eating it."

Steph took a generous bite of her own slice. Yep, this was pretty darn good. "I can't call it tofu pot pie, though; nobody will want to even try it."

"True, true." Lynne chuckled. "Just call it Savory Lemongrass Pie or something. Is it vegan?"

"No, there's butter in the crust. It is vegetarian, though."

"You could make it vegan if you needed to, right?"

"I could."

They both sat chewing contentedly, polishing off their slices of the Savory Lemongrass Pie. "Wow," Lynne said again, pushing her empty plate away and glancing ruefully at her first three plates before looking back over at Steph. "Why do you torture me like this?"

Steph laughed again. "You don't have to finish those now—I'll send them home with you in a container. I got what I needed to know here."

"What are you figuring this all out for, anyway? We don't have a neighborhood association meeting coming up. Are you throwing another party?"

"Oh, it's just for a side thing for my next soup group here. Yes, you don't have to tell me that it got completely out of hand, I know it did."

"Good, then I won't." Lynne eyed the lamb pie, bringing the plate a little closer to herself and picking up her fork but not—yet—taking another bite.

"It's just, I noticed that my date is March 14, and it got me thinking."

Lynne looked at her blankly. "Okay?"

"Pi day—pie day! Three-one-four!"

"Oh, for heaven's sake…" They both laughed together. "Steph, you are a wonder. It's too bad Kate doesn't have food shows at her gallery, you'd make a fortune." Steph shook her head. Lynne went on: "And it is too bad you don't want to run a restaurant. We're so privileged to be able to eat your magical creations, but I feel like your talents are wasted on us."

"You're worth it! And I do have other friends over—I mean, we do. And David loves my cooking. Besides, it's fun. You're right: it's my art, but I don't have any kind of urge to share it more widely."

"Are you certain about that?" Lynne pressed. "I know your life is in good order, and you guys certainly don't need any more money, but Steph, dear, I saw you at your Christmas party. You were entirely alive then. You do seem happy enough now, but there's a whole side of your personality that really needs to feed a crowd—that gets validation and satisfaction from it."

"Well, you're not wrong," Steph allowed. "I do like seeing a big group of people enjoying what I've done. But it's a ton of work."

"And I would never push you into doing work you don't want to do," Lynne said. "But—well, I'm just going to be blunt: you're bored, my friend. In my completely non-expert opinion, you actually do need some work to do. Not a tedious job—I know you had one of those for decades, and gladly gave it up—but you need a calling, a mission."

Above and beyond repairing my marriage—yet again? she thought. But she hadn't talked to Lynne about this since telling her that all was well, and she didn't want to get into it again until she had a better idea of where things were going. "We've talked before about the dangers of turning a beloved hobby into a job…"

Lynne shook her head. "Yes, and this is not that. Again, you're so fortunate in that you do not need to earn a living. You don't even need to make back your expenses, if you decide you want to just throw a big community party once every quarter or whatever. But Steph," she said, pointing at her with her fork, "I think you need some structure and outside responsibility in order to feel fulfilled, and I think if that responsibility doesn't involve feeding people, then the world will be a darker place."

Steph laughed. "Yikes!"

Lynne was unrepentant. "I'm not even kidding here. You and Julie helped me so much the other day, and I'm taking seriously my mission to return the favor—with more than just choosing which of four pot pies to make for some friends in a few weeks. You obviously want to cook amazing food for people, and you're better at it than anyone I've ever met, not to mention ninety-nine-point-nine percent of the restaurants I've ever eaten in. I'm arguing that you should lean into that."

"More than just the entertaining and soup groups that I already do?"

"Yes, absolutely. Steph, I know it's crass, but people value things they pay for. If you did occasional ticketed dinners…do you remember the group dinners at Red Rabbit Farm?"

"Oh yes. Those were amazing, and so much fun."

"You could do something like that. Yes, you'd have to find a venue—I know you don't have a big field for parking and a sweet outbuilding where you can seat forty or fifty people—but that's the easy part. I could even ask around and find a place, I'm sure."

Steph smiled. "What's the hard part?"

"Convincing you that this is a good idea," Lynne said, without missing a beat. "That you need to feel engaged in something, and connected to a regular rhythm that isn't just a group of friends having dinner every couple of weeks. Not that that's a bad thing—it's a great thing. I'm just saying, it isn't enough."

Everything Lynne was saying made sense, Steph thought, and even sounded like fun. So why did she feel so resistant to this? *Did* she feel resistant, or was her brain simply still trying to wrap itself around the idea? "Those Red Rabbit dinners were spendy," she said, after a minute. "I remember meeting wealthy tourists from Seattle at those things—nice people, but it was kind of exclusive, you know?"

"True. Again, you wouldn't need to charge anything, but remember what I said about what people value…"

"I could do a sliding scale," Steph said, leaning forward as the concept began to take shape in her mind. "And—no tourists. This would be for locals only, and no islander would be turned away for lack of means. We've got other pay-what-you-can-afford things here—even the Orcas Center has three or four different prices on their tickets, and you choose what to pay."

"Exactly!" Lynne's eyes shone. "This is just what I'm talking about! A recurring, periodic thing—not very often at first, till you see how it goes, how you like it—but one that builds community."

"There was that winter reading series at the winery, with all the candles," Steph said, remembering. "Those were really great, and I saw a lot of the same people at each one."

"And there were only three or four all winter, right?" Lynne asked. "Definitely doable."

Steph leaned back, wishing she had her laptop, or even a notebook and pen. "You've given me a lot to think about…"

Lynne laughed and got to her feet, making Steph realize that somehow, she'd polished off all four of her pieces of pie without

Steph even noticing. No need to hunt for a container. "Marvelous! I've lit a fire in you, I can see that. *Now* I feel like I've returned your favor, and can let you get on with the rest of your day."

Steph laughed as well, and got up to walk Lynne to the door. "I'm going to begin by researching what sorts of venues might be available for renting, and what's involved with that."

"I am happy to help with that, as I said."

"Thanks." Then she rolled her eyes. "David would hate these dinners."

"He doesn't have to go to them! Again, think of them as your work that you love. You don't sit beside him at his computer and analyze foreign stock markets, do you?"

"Good god, no."

"So just because your 'work' might be in the hospitality field, that doesn't mean he needs to be a part of it. Quite the opposite, in fact. Look at Ethan: coming up here for the weekend because Marie's restaurant is involved in some big thing. She wants him out of her hair, not pretending that they're attending it together as guests."

"Right." Steph nodded, and then pulled her friend into a quick hug. "Thank you, Lynne, so much. This is great."

"It was my pleasure." She patted her belly. "*All* of it was my pleasure. I can't wait for the mid-March soup group! What ever am I going to make for mine on Sunday? Jeez, I can't believe it's already upon us."

"Whatever you do, it'll be great. I never want any of you to feel like I'm being competitive or anything—"

"We don't, don't worry," Lynne assured her. "We all love you, Steph, *and* your cooking—and we're happy you are willing to eat our cooking in return." She winked. "Anything to stay on your good side."

Steph blew her a kiss and shut the door as Lynne headed down the path between their houses.

Back in her kitchen, she put away the uneaten portions of pie, loaded all eight plates and forks into the dishwasher, and went to her computer.

Time to do some research.

RON

HE SET THE pen down and leaned back, looking with some astonishment at the growing pile of manuscript pages on his desk.

Ron had never been able to compose on a computer. Typing just didn't feel like writing to him—it felt like the second step, the work that was done after the creative act of the writing itself. So he still wrote all his books longhand.

In the olden days, it was easy to find a girl to type up handwritten pages—for little or no pay, especially if she was a girl who was sweet on you (whether or not you were sweet on her in return). Yes, women used to be called girls, though Ron was intelligent enough to only do so in the privacy of his own head anymore.

He would have to type these pages up himself, alas. He kept thinking he would get to the typing after the end of a chapter... but then he ended up diving into the next chapter instead.

Ron was also smart enough to not interrupt the muse when she was barking at him like this. Let the words flow; typing could come later.

He had no idea what to make of this book, however. Not only wasn't it one of his usual literary studies...it wasn't even scholarly. It was *fiction*, of all things.

Ron read very little contemporary fiction, of course. In fact he read very little classic fiction either anymore; he read other scholars' literary studies about classic fiction, and articles and reviews of same—keeping up with the field, even though he was retired. Because old academics never truly retired, not until they were six feet under. As long as there was one more article to be written, one more journal to read, one more critique to produce, one more conference to attend, the work was never done.

He had started this book, in fact, thinking he was writing a journal article. It had begun in the usual way of his writing: with a disorganized dump of thoughts, a stream-of-consciousness flow of getting the words out onto paper, to be sorted through, analyzed, and arranged later.

Only after he'd written twenty or thirty-odd pages did he realize that half these thoughts weren't scholarly, exactly. They were ruminative, emotional, self-examining...they weren't a journal article, they were journal*ing*.

Ron had never journaled in all his life. When he emerged from the fugue of creation and saw what he'd done, he'd set the project aside in disgust for a few weeks, though he didn't throw the pages away; he just glared at them whenever he went into his study for something else.

That was just before the ill-fated Christmas party-slumber party. About which the less said, the better.

A few weeks into the new year, however, Ron again found himself in his study, and this time he pulled the stack of pages from the corner of the desk and sat down, reading them through.

They weren't bad.

Oh, of course, they were badly overwritten: maudlin, jejune, excessively emotional and overwrought, even repetitive in places; but underneath all the dross there were some reasonably insightful truths...and they were connected at their heart by a powerful query: what makes a modern enlightened man, and what is the responsibility of this enlightened man to share his insights and wisdom with others?

So, despite his deep-seated suspicion of the whole idea of writing fiction, he picked the pen back up and resumed work.

Naturally, when he eventually typed it up, he would have to change it all from first person to third person, but just knowing that he was going to do this was unexpectedly freeing. Since this wasn't meant to be a journal (shudder) or a memoir or autobiography of any kind, since it was patently *not about himself*, Ron was not constrained by the need to write literal truths, or put incidents in exact chronological order or anything like that. He could write the deeper truths, confident in the knowledge that he was crafting a story.

And what was the story about? Oh, he'd figure out the intricacies of the plot later, if he actually decided he truly wanted to go through with this, write the requisite number of words and secure a publisher and all that; but the *story* he was telling was one of a man displaced. A man who worked hard all his life, followed all the generally accepted paths and milestones, a man who was not only intelligent but diligent and honest and well-grounded, a man who was born and bred to be a leader...who suddenly found himself in a changed world. A world with no place for him to stand, no role for him to inhabit. A world that had not violently rejected him or anything, but instead had somehow just... meandered on ahead, leaving him and everything he knew and valued in the dust.

Which was even worse than having been violently rejected, to his way of thinking. To be battled, even if you ultimately lose, is still to be valued, to be taken seriously. To be *respected*. But to be simply shrugged off, ignored? As if you were irrelevant? That brought a deep and bitter pain.

But this man was not bitter! No, Ron had no interest in rehashing that whiny old story. This man, who was *not* Ron, knew (as did Ron) that everything and everyone has a season, and that it is the natural way of things for the elders to rise in the esteem of their peers and underlings...but only to a point, after which the elders begin, naturally, to recede. To give up their place at the head of the line, to step aside and make room for the young Turks.

This story would be the rational, relaxed, contemplative story of a man who has been an acknowledged leader, admired and respected by everyone he encounters, who wisely, sagely discerns the precise moment at which he must step aside, handing off the reins of power and authority to others...who discerns this moment so well, so intuitively, so gently yet (yes) authoritatively that he cannot help but be even *more greatly* esteemed by all who encounter him.

Yet, of course, he is so humble and so wise that, when the acolytes and the young Turks alike beg him to retain his position just a little longer, to teach them everything he knows, to lead them by his continued example, he graciously and gracefully refuses. "You are ready," he says to one and all who implore him not to leave them in the lurch. "We are not ready!" they cry—literal tears, sometimes, sparkling at the corners of their sincere, pleading eyes. "This is how I know you are," he says to them, laying a firm but gentle hand upon their shoulders. "No one who is actually ready to step up believes themselves to be ready." He feels answering tears gathering in his own eyes, gratitude and humility in his heart, and a strong sense of rectitude. "Go and do well. I believe in you, my friend."

Or something like that. He'd sort of lost the thread there, and maybe some of his points contradicted each other, but it would all get cleaned up in the rewriting. And of course, it would all be told so much more subtly in the actual novel. There would have to be some drama and setbacks and crap like that added in, just to keep the readers interested.

Ron didn't want his novel to be heavy-handed.

But of course, it wouldn't be. He wouldn't let it be.

At one point, years ago, he would have asked Alicia to read over some of his chapters—after his initial edit and polish, of course—to get her point of view, her perspective. But there was no way he was going to share this project with her. Not only would she not understand what he was trying to do here—he was quite certain she would discern the personal elements underneath the narrative, no matter how carefully he tried to disguise them; she would completely misinterpret his intentions—but her very *seriousness* had become sorely lacking in recent years. Yes, she had always been a children's book editor; but only recently had he realized that she herself thought in a juvenile way. She was all about the appetites and delights of the moment—gallivanting off to play that stupid whiffleball game with her friends; adding too much cream to the soup; dumping exquisite French wine on slices of *toast*—and had entirely let go of the groundedness and maturity that had attracted him to her in the first place, despite her age.

She had seemed the perfect partner, when they'd met. She was lovely and lively, while also being serious and intellectual. Most irresistibly, she had been interested in him but not *too* interested; he had had to woo her; she had not been like previous girlfriends of his after the divorce, clinging like limpets far too soon in their romance, sighing and making cow eyes at every jewelry store they passed. Alicia had been…warm yet cool. Just slightly elusive, and so he'd had to have her, and, ultimately, have her he did.

It had been good for a long time.

They had balanced each other. They had understood each other. They had, he thought, respected each other.

And now? He never caught her at it, but Ron had the overwhelming sense that after anything he said, she would roll her eyes. If he told her that he was going to work on something that required focused concentration, she would bring out the vacuum cleaner and run it right outside his office door—even thumping it into the door a few times, as if for good measure. If he asked her to make dinner in time to eat by six, she would linger in town with her friends until five fifty-five, then saunter home and slap something together that he didn't even like. If he threw her a bone and suggested they watch an episode of that stupid TV show she liked after dinner, she had to vanish into her own office to work on some sudden "rush" freelance job until bedtime.

It was no wonder he found his thoughts roaming toward sweet, gentle Steph.

Too bad, but no wonder.

Ron sighed, refocusing on the pad of paper in front of him, the pen in his hand. He was mortified to see that he'd been doodling on the page, writing "Steph" over and over again. He tore the paper off the pad, crumpled it up—too bad about the manuscript words lost, but he could reconstruct them—and tossed it into the trash can beside his desk.

A minute later, he got up and retrieved the crumpled paper, stuffing it in his pocket. He'd put it in the fireplace. In fact he'd do it right now: that would be just what he needed, to have Alicia somehow stumble across this egregious artifact in his pocket.

He stacked the manuscript pages neatly and laid the pen atop them before walking over and opening his office door, looking up and down the hallway, listening carefully. He didn't hear anything, though that could mean she was quietly working in her own study, or wasting more good wine in some harebrained kitchen project, or any number of other things. He just didn't know what she got up to with her time these days.

In the great room, he was relieved to find the kitchen empty. He went straight to the fireplace, tossed in the damning evidence, and piled more fire-starting waste paper on top of it, with cardboard and kindling over that. In minutes, he had a lovely blaze going.

"Oh, that's nice," Alicia said, appearing as if by magic in the room behind him. She didn't have a jacket or purse; she must have been in the house somewhere.

"Yes, I thought it was getting a little chilly." He gave her a strained smile. Did he look guilty? He hoped he didn't look guilty. He had nothing to be guilty about. He had nothing to hide.

"Are you done working for the day?" She walked over to the kitchen island and thumbed through the pile of mail, setting it back down again unopened.

"I am," he decided. "Shall we have a glass of wine?"

"That sounds perfect." She gave him a genuine-looking smile with no eye rolling. "I'll put a platter of cheese and stuff together and meet you back here."

He nodded, thinking *"cheese and stuff"* *indeed*, and headed for the wine cellar.

Chapter 7

MATT

G ordon hated the full-spectrum lamp.

He said it hurt his eyes; he said he couldn't figure out how to turn it on; he said it was a waste of costly electricity; he said it made a buzzing sound that bothered his ears (though Matt couldn't hear it).

Choose your battles, went the saying, and Matt did not want to fight this one.

The problem was, Gordon also didn't want to do his exercises, and he didn't want to eat anything but candy and chips, and he didn't want to get out of his recliner in front of the TV, and he *really* didn't want to drink water.

"I'm not sure what to do exactly," Matt told Lynne, as they prepped for her soup group meeting. He'd called and offered to come over early to help her, and when she'd told him she had it all under control, he'd admitted that he actually wanted to talk to a doctor, but not *Gordon's* doctor. He just wanted a reality check from a knowledgeable source, not actual medical advice.

After warning him that her son Ethan would also be in the house, Lynne had told him that he was more than welcome to come early, and still wouldn't need to help.

He found a way to pitch in, though, chopping celery and cabbage for one of Lynne's beloved slaw-style salads as he told her what was going on. "Do I push him harder to do the things that will keep him healthier, or do I let him live his life how he wants to? I mean, what's the end game here? He's going to lose more of his memory, and eventually he's going to die. Should I just let him make his own decisions?" He grabbed a bunch of radishes and brought them to the sink to wash. "I mean, within reason, of course."

"Yes, of course," Lynne said with an understanding chuckle. "You don't want to hand him the car keys and send him to the grocery store, no matter how sure he is that he's still a great driver who will remember the whole grocery list."

"Exactly." He scrubbed the radishes and brought them back to his cutting board.

Lynne stirred the fragrant soup on the stove, then replaced its lid. "I'm afraid I don't have a terribly satisfying answer for you."

Matt shrugged. "I suspected as much."

"The trouble with many dementias is that they're a moving target—and not only do they not move at an even pace, they don't even move in a straight line. Things can go backwards, and then abruptly forward again; you can settle into a new 'normal' for a while and then everything changes again without warning." Matt was nodding along with her words. "I'm not telling you anything you don't already know all too well," Lynne went on. "But that's the complication: the answer to 'what should you do' is going to keep moving too, especially as he struggles to hang onto whatever autonomy and independence he can. If he fights you hard on one thing, like the lamp, then I'd say let it go, and see if you can get him to do another healthy thing as a trade, like drink a whole glass of water. Try it for a few days in a row—and give that up too if it's a non-starter."

"So I shouldn't just give up entirely, is what you're saying. I should keep encouraging healthier living."

Lynne sighed. "I'd say yes? If you can? If it's not making both of you miserable."

"It's hard to say," Matt said, dropping the radishes into the big salad bowl. "And to be completely honest, I don't know how much of our struggle is coming from me—from *my* need to hang onto my authority or whatever, as his caregiver. Or even to just have a system figured out and be able to stick to it. The shifting landscape, it's really hard."

"Yes, it really is," Lynne said, her voice filled with empathy. "It's why memory care facilities are so rigidly rule- and schedule-bound, and why they strike so many people as such unpleasant places. They *have* to control their severely cognitively impaired patients for their own protection, and those patients will never comprehend why this is happening to them."

"I hope Gordon never has to be in such a place," Matt said. "He certainly doesn't need that level of care now, but I don't know how it unfolds from here—or even when I'll know, exactly. With the moving target, there's probably going to be one day when I think, *Oh, I can't handle him here anymore*, and then the next he'll seem totally fine to stay in my house."

"There's going to be many of those days, actually," Lynne said. "It's not going to be a clean decision, if you know what I mean."

"I'll always be second-guessing?"

"Exactly. There may come a day when you realize there have been too many dangerous or difficult experiences at home, over too long a time, to keep him there safely anymore, and that you really do need to move him to an institution. But then he'll likely keep having some of the 'he seems totally fine at home' days sprinkled in among the 'he can't stay at home' days. It'll be a challenge to keep your perspective then." She gave him a gentle smile. "Feel free to talk to me about this then, too, and I'll remind you of this conversation, and of the difficult days—of the reason you're making the decision you'll need to make."

"Thank you, Lynne." He shrugged again. "I don't know if I find it encouraging or discouraging that it's only going to get worse from here."

Now her smile was rueful. "I can't even give you a platitude like 'it might not!' Because you're right: the end game here is that Gordon continues to lose his faculties, and either he dies at home, or you have to put him in a care facility so he can die there. But that doesn't mean you can't do something more, or different, with the time you have now. He still enjoys social gatherings, right?"

"He does. It's the only time he really seems to perk up."

"Why don't you bring him to these dinners? He's more than welcome here, you know."

"Oh, well, I don't want to burden everyone with him…"

"Matt." Lynne put down her knife and held his gaze. "Everyone loves him, and they love *you*. You're our friend, and he's your father. Yes, he asks the same questions over and over again, and he dotes on the ladies—especially Julie. *Nobody minds that.* He's a sweetheart, and we can see how much he enjoys himself in a gathering. And if it takes a moment of the burden off of you, I know we would all feel even more strongly about wanting you to bring him."

"Thank you." He felt unexpectedly emotional at her words. "I appreciate that, more than you can know."

"But?" she asked, with a perceptive smile.

"Well, I work at home, you know. I take him to the senior center for things, and I take him to his doctor's appointments, and I'm with him all day and all night…" Lynne was nodding; she got it, but he went ahead and said it anyway: "These evenings are kind of my only break. I really need to be able to get out and be with—I want to say 'grownups,' which is telling, if kind of cruel."

"It's not cruel, and I know exactly what you mean," Lynne assured him.

"Plus, Ramona counts on the income," Matt added. "Yes, I know I could still hire her to stay with him on other nights, or even to come be with him while I'm home and just trying to get some work done, but—well, this is what we've got set up now, and it's working. And I really do love these evenings with you guys. *Alone* with you guys." He laughed. "Even if what I do with that alone time is talk about Dad."

"Hey Mom?" Ethan called from the living room.

"One second," Lynne said to Matt, and then, louder, "Yes?"

"I'm heading out." He appeared in the kitchen doorway. "I shouldn't be too late."

"Wait, what?" Lynne asked. "Where are you going? The rest of the soup group is going to be here in a few minutes."

"Levon texted, we're gonna meet up at the Lower for a burger. Sorry! I haven't seen him in ages."

"But I told everyone you were going to be here! We set a place for you."

Ethan gave her a sympathetic look. "I know, but they're your friends. Nobody cares about seeing me."

Lynne looked like she wanted to argue back again, but then she sighed. "Okay. Have fun."

"Thanks!" And then he was gone; Matt heard the front door slam, followed by the sound of a car starting.

Lynne shook her head and resumed chopping cilantro.

"Do you want me to reset the table?" Matt asked after a minute, breaking the suddenly strained silence.

"If you like." She turned to him with a look of frustration. "You'd never know he was in his mid-thirties, would you?"

Not all that much younger than me, Matt thought. *Though I can't remember ever running out on my mom when she was throwing a dinner party and expecting me to be there.* "Is Levon one of his friends from high school?"

"Exactly. I shouldn't let it bother me—now we can have the evening we were going to have before he decided to come up this weekend. And he did spend a lot of time with his old mom."

"Well, you might as well appreciate what you've got—while you can still remember how old he is."

She smiled then, but it was a sad smile. "Yeah. Perspective. Thanks, Matt."

"That's me: always good as a cautionary tale!"

Lynne abruptly set her knife down and walked over to Matt. "Hug?"

"Hug," he agreed instantly, and stepped into her arms.

JULIE

GAVIN CAME ALONG to this soup group as well, which was nice. He even brought a dish, which Julie had told him he didn't have to, but he'd wanted to. They'd learned that Lynne was planning something Mexican-flavored, so he baked cornbread.

"My famous cornbread," he'd told Julie.

"What's famous about it?" she'd asked.

"It's just the best cornbread you've ever had, that's all."

Whatever made it famous, or best, it certainly did smell good. Julie hadn't had much to eat yet today—she'd gotten busy working on stuff in her studio in an attempt to distract herself from worrying about being evicted from her own damn house, and lost track of the time—so it was kind of making her crazy. "Are you sure we can't just sneak a little corner of a bite out of that?" she asked Gavin, glancing over at him before returning her eyes to the road.

He laughed, holding the pan just a little farther away from her. "You see, my love, the thing about making food that comes in a single solid shape is that one cannot disturb the shape without everyone knowing. I begin to see the wisdom of *soup* dinners— one can sneak as much soup as one wants, and as long as there's some left, nobody is any the wiser."

"Except in our soup group, the host makes the soup. It's hard to sneak something out of Lynne's kitchen while I am still driving to her house."

"True. Perhaps I should have made something like Matt's cheese straws. While those do have a shape, they can be rearranged in their container to cover any evidence of missing straws."

Julie groaned theatrically. "Can we talk about something else? I'm going to pass out from hunger. And yes, before you point out that I brought it up, smartypants, I know I did. I plead temporary insanity by virtue of starvation."

"All right," Gavin said. "Want to talk about our new book group?"

"Really?" Julie perked up. "Are things actually coalescing?"

"Maybe. I've had some signups on the sheet I put out at the library, and also I think my friend Will might be interested."

"Do I know Will?"

"You met him once—that day last fall when you and your friends were playing pickleball."

"Oh!" Julie just managed to prevent herself from saying *The silver fox!* "I remember him, yes, but I didn't really talk to him. You guys and Lynne went out for beers afterward, I think."

"We did, that's right."

Julie chuckled. "So, he reads women's fiction? Or are we not starting with Libby Perrine books after all?"

Gavin laughed as well. "He says he's open to reading anything—that a story is a story, and if it's well told, he's there for it."

"Well, he's right about that. So what does he do? Tell me more about him." Julie's stomach chose this moment to growl loud enough for Gavin to hear, even over the noise of the engine.

"Wow!" he said. "We have really got to get you something to eat!"

"I was fine until I started smelling your cornbread. Is it still warm from the oven? Why does it smell so insanely good?"

"If you want to pull over, I can put it in the trunk."

"No, that's fine. We'll be there in a few minutes, and Lynne will have something I can snack on."

"If you say so." He shifted the pan a little farther away from her. As if she was going to grab at it while she was driving. It was a tempting thought. "You asked about Will, though," Gavin went on. "He's semi-retired, and he doesn't live on the island full-time—he spends part of the year in Arizona."

"Which is probably why I don't know him, huh?" Julie asked. She'd met Gavin's neighbors, with whom he was friendly, and a number of his coworkers at the library; he didn't seem to have a huge social circle, but he wasn't a weird loner or anything.

"Exactly. After that pickleball game, he hasn't really been around. But he's back now for a few months."

"And he wants to join a book group in a place where he only lives part-time?"

"He does, if we'll have him. But I did want to ask you how you feel about that. Would it work, or do you want the continuity of having people committed year-round?"

Julie thought about it a moment. "I'm open to giving it a try. When I've had book groups in the past, there's always someone who can't make a meeting. This would just be something we'd adjust to, especially if he generally is gone on some sort of pre-dictable schedule?"

"He is—he winters down there, mostly, and lives here spring through fall. Mostly."

"I know the usual thing to say is that that must be nice," Julie said, "but honestly, he's missing out. I've really grown to love our winters here."

"I'm with you. You can try to persuade him at our first meeting—which leads to my next question: how often do we want to meet, and on which night of the week? I assume these are night-time meetings."

"Yes, I think, evenings—and I guess we have to figure out if they include dinner or not." She frowned. The soup groups, be-ing potlucks twice a month, already made for a lot of cooking and entertaining. Which she enjoyed, of course, but they were also some work.

Gavin glanced over at her. "We could have them in a public

setting that serves food—or, since that could be noisy and expensive, we could use one of the library's rooms and pick up pizzas and drinks and stuff."

"Could we do that, eat in the library? I like that idea."

"Sure—we have all sorts of events that include food and drink."

"Cool." Julie slowed down as they entered the twenty-five-mile-an-hour zone in Deer Harbor. "As for days of the week—well, not Sundays. I don't have strong feelings about the other days. We can see what the members think, when we have members."

"Makes sense. I can also check when the library meeting rooms are reliably free."

"That's great, thank you." It was so terribly sweet that he was engaged with this. Yes, it was part of his Grand Romantic Gesture which had convinced her that he understood he'd screwed up and that he truly did want her in his life; but they'd been doing great since then. A less wonderful man might relax a bit once the crisis had passed...might not keep the project of organizing a book group to read women's fiction at the top of his priority list.

Julie was beginning to suspect that Gavin actually was as thoughtful and loving as he seemed.

They were nearly at Lynne's house by now. A small, bright yellow car passed them going the other direction. "Was that Ethan? Lynne's son?" Julie asked, watching the car grow smaller in her rearview mirror.

"I don't know, never met him," Gavin said.

"She'd said he was going to be at the meeting tonight—she seemed excited about that."

"Maybe she needed something last-minute from the store."

"Yeah, maybe." There was a tiny market at the Deer Harbor marina. "Anyway, here we are."

After parking, they ran into Steph arriving at the same time, walking over from her house next door with a picnic basket full of undoubtedly wonderful treats. "Hey guys," Steph said. "How are things?"

"Starving," Julie said. "Things are starving. What do you have in there?"

Steph laughed and reached into the basket. "Here—think of it as a bite-sized bagel dog."

Julie stuffed the savory delight into her mouth. "Oh my god, will you marry me?"

"Hey!" Gavin mock-protested.

Steph handed Julie a second meaty morsel. "Wait 'til you taste them with the sauce," she said, and knocked on Lynne's door.

Once inside, Gavin followed Steph into the kitchen with his cornbread while Julie sat on the living room couch next to Matt. "Alicia just called," he told her; "she and Ron are running a little late. They'll be here in about ten minutes."

"What, did he get lost in his wine cellar?" Julie asked with a smile.

"Probably decided it needed a full reorganization, or he needed to order seventeen new cases of some rare vintage. Whatever it was, I'm sure he'll make it clear to everyone that it was Alicia's fault."

She and Matt shared an uncomfortable, knowing smile. Yeah, she wasn't the only one who had noticed the increasing tension there.

She changed the subject. "I thought I saw Lynne's son on the road—did she run out of something for the soup?"

"No, he got a call from an old high school buddy and bailed on us old folks."

"Oh, that's too bad." Julie gave a rueful smile. "Though that sounds like something my girls would do, honestly. It's a good thing they didn't go to high school here—I can generally keep them around when they visit."

Matt gave her an unreadable look as Lynne came out into the living room with a platter of appetizers: Steph's bagel bites with the promised sauce; chopped veggies with several other dipping sauces; and corn chips with guacamole. "I know you did chips and guac last time," she said to Matt, "but with tortilla soup, I pretty much had no choice."

"No complaints here!" Julie said, loading up a chip and stuffing it in her mouth. "Though I'm so hungry, I'd better be careful to leave some room for the actual meal." She took a second chip and then nudged the platter closer to Matt.

Gavin came out as Lynne went back into the kitchen. "Whoo, girl talk in there," he said with a grin, sitting beside Juile on the couch. He reached out and pulled the platter closer to himself— and right back in front of her.

"Girl talk?" she asked, trying to resist taking another of Steph's bagel things, then realizing that she really did need to try one with the sauce. Hey, she didn't make the rules here. She grabbed one, dipped it, and popped it in her mouth. Heavenly.

"Yeah, I was getting my cornbread in the oven to keep it warm and they were whispering about something. It had to do with men being disappointing, I guess. So I thought that was my cue to head out here."

"Lynne's probably disappointed that Ethan isn't spending the evening with us," Julie said.

"Oh, he isn't?" Gavin took a bagel bite, dipped it, and chewed it thoughtfully. "Wow, these are good. Steph really can cook. Has she ever thought about opening a restaurant?"

Matt and Julie both laughed. "Don't mention that to her," Julie said. "She's very tired of hearing it."

"Yeah," Matt added. "She's made it really, really clear that all her joy in cooking comes from it *not* being her job."

"That's fair."

Lynne came out of the kitchen with an open bottle of white wine in one hand, and three empty wine glasses in the other. "Is everyone okay with Pinot Grigio, or do you guys want to wait till Mr. Red Wine gets here? This is all I have."

"White looks great," Julie said.

Gavin shook his head. "I probably won't have wine tonight.

I'm already drinking way more than I used to, since I took up with this bad influence here." He gave Julie a fond glance and a nudge. "And I did promise to drive us back to town."

"That's fine," Lynne said. "Can I get you something else?" She set all three glasses on the coffee table.

"No, I'm good for now."

"Matt?" she asked.

"White's fine with me," he said.

She poured their two glasses and took the bottle back to the kitchen.

When Ron and Alicia arrived fifteen or twenty minutes later, Alicia immediately headed into the kitchen while Ron stood in the living room, looking askance at the half-empty glasses of white. "What in the world are you drinking?"

Julie looked up at him. "The wine that was served to us by our hostess, which actually goes beautifully with these yummy appetizers. What have you brought?"

But she almost instantly tuned out his answer, focusing instead on the voices in the kitchen. Alicia sounded distressed; Lynne's and Steph's voices were quieter, but sounded as though they were soothing her. What was going on? "I'll be right back," Julie said, getting up and brushing past a surprised Ron on her way to the kitchen.

Alicia was standing by the sink, wiping her eyes with a hand towel. She shook her head and gave Julie a watery smile. "I'm fine—just a momentary wobble."

Both Lynne and Steph were standing beside her, looking concerned. "Do you want to sit down?" Steph asked her, indicating a chair at the kitchen table.

Alicia nodded and stepped over to the chair, dropping down into it. "Truly, I'm okay now. Just…sometimes his anxiety pushes my buttons."

His anxiety? Is that what you call it? Julie thought, taking the seat next to Alicia. "Do you want to talk about it?" She glanced over at Lynne, who just shook her head and turned back to her soup.

"It wouldn't do any good, and would only bring the evening down." Alicia took a deep breath. "We get together to have fun!"

"We get together because we're friends," Steph put in gently, also coming over to the table. "Friends who care about each other. Nobody shut Matt down last fall and ordered him to be cheerful when he told us that Heather had hopped onto a ferry, never to return."

Alicia gave her a grateful look, and opened her mouth to say something, but Ron walked into the kitchen holding his usual fancy wine-caddy. "Lynne, I need an opener stat. They're drinking supermarket Pinot Grigio out there."

He really is getting worse, Julie thought. *Or was he always this way, only now we're all just completely over it?* It was hard to tell. A charming curmudgeon was one thing; a cranky asshole was something else altogether.

The cranky asshole who made his wife cry on the way to dinner with friends…

Without a word, Lynne opened a drawer and pulled out a corkscrew, handing it to Ron. If he noticed the uncomfortable air in the kitchen, he didn't let on.

"Thanks," he said, setting the wine-caddy on the counter and pulling out a bottle.

While he was opening it, Alicia got up and left the room. Lynne's house was nearly as small as Julie's, so Julie could see from where she was sitting that Alicia walked straight through the living room, where Matt and Gavin were chatting, and headed for the bathroom in the hall.

Julie wondered if she should follow her; she looked a question at Steph, hoping for silent guidance.

Steph shrugged. "I think it's okay for now," she said softly. "I can check on her in a bit."

The sound of a cork leaving a bottle filled the kitchen. "I hope you have enough clean glasses," Ron said to Lynne.

I hope Lynne dumps the pot of hot soup over his head, Julie thought, and said to Steph, "I'm going to the living room before all your amazing bagel bites are gone."

After retaking her seat beside Gavin, Julie kept an eye on the bathroom door. Alicia eventually emerged, looking better, and took a chair next to the sofa.

"Hey," Julie said to her, softly. "You okay?"

"Yeah, it's—no biggie," Alicia said. "Maybe hormones."

Hormones? Julie thought. *Ron's hormones?*

Ron walked in from the kitchen holding two full glasses of red wine. "You need one," he said to Gavin.

"No, thanks," Gavin said, but Ron set one before him anyway.

"I'll drink it," Julie whispered to Gavin. She hadn't finished her Pinot Grigio, but Ron wouldn't let her use her same glass for the red, so she might as well. Once his back was turned, she discreetly took a sip of the new wine. It was delicious, of course. Ron might be an ass, but he did know his wines.

After a few minutes, everyone had found a seat in the cozy living room. "Tell the gang the latest with McLeod," Steph prompted her.

"Oh jeez!" Julie said, running a hand through her hair. "You guys are not going to believe this…"

"It sure sounds personal to me," Matt said, when she had finished. "Does anyone else live behind their shop on any of those streets?"

"I think there's an apartment above Darvill's," Julie said, "but I don't know if anyone's living in it right now."

"And there's that little house on Prune Alley," Alicia said. "Close to the bike rental place."

"What little house?" Ron asked. "I don't know any little house."

"With the weird windows?"

Matt laughed suddenly. "Oh, you mean the building that used to be the escape room? That's not a house."

"It looks like one," Alicia said.

"Spookiest house ever!" Matt said. He turned to Julie and Gavin. "It sounds like we've got more research to do: we need to find out who might be on the wrong side of these new 'regulations,' and come up with a plan to resist them together."

Gavin chuckled. "Do the commission's inspection before they even get to it? I like it."

"Anything is better than sitting around waiting for the next shoe to drop," Julie agreed.

They spent a while strategizing, with most of the group volunteering to talk to at least a few business owners, gathering all the information they could about how everyone used their commercial spaces. Julie felt better all the time as her friends rallied around her like this.

Finally, she took the last bagel bite. "Ugh, I was so hungry, and now I'm full."

"Well," Lynne said with a smile, "shall we eat dinner then?"

STEPH

EVEN RON BEING in extra-jerk mode wasn't enough to ruin the nice evening, she thought, as she helped Lynne with some of the cleanup before heading home. She had texted David when the rest of the guests left, seeing if he was waiting for her or if she could stay another twenty minutes or so. He hadn't answered, which either meant he was deep into whatever he was doing, or he was already asleep.

She was loading bowls into the dishwasher when Lynne's cell phone rang, out in the living room. "I've got this," Steph assured her, so Lynne went and answered it.

She returned to the kitchen a minute later, frowning.

"Everything all right?" Steph asked.

"I don't know. That was—"

Before she finished her sentence, they both heard the front

door opening and closing. Ethan came into the kitchen, accompanied by the strong smell of cigarette smoke, and maybe something else underneath it. "Hey," he said, dropping his backpack on the table. "Your group all gone?"

"Yes," Lynne said. "Marie just called, looking for you. She couldn't get you on your phone."

"I was driving."

"She said she called you an hour ago as well."

"Huh." He seemed unconcerned. "I'll call her in a bit."

Steph kept rinsing and loading dishes, wondering if she should make her exit.

After a minute, Lynne said, "How was Levon?"

Ethan shrugged; in that moment, he looked about sixteen to Steph, though she knew he was in his thirties. "I dunno. He kinda…isn't moving. You know?"

"Not really. Moving how, or where?"

Ethan went to the fridge and opened it, staring inside for a long moment before pulling out the nearly-finished bottle of Pinot Grigio. "Can I have this?"

"Of course," Lynne said, moving automatically to get him a wine glass.

He grabbed a tumbler from the cupboard next to the fridge. "This is cool, I don't need a fancy glass." He unscrewed the cap and dumped the wine into the tumbler, then went and dropped into a chair at the table. "He's, well, still here. Still working at the grocery store."

This wasn't her conversation—or her son, for that matter—but Steph felt a surge of protective indignation hearing this. "Nothing wrong with working at a grocery store. And the Island Market is amazing—they treat their employees marvelously."

Ethan turned his gaze on her with another shrug. "I don't mean that like how it sounded; I just, well, Levon was one of the smartest kids in our class. He had ideas, he was gonna go places. But he didn't. He's living with his folks, and he's got the same job he had right out of high school, and he's still seeing Shayla on and off, and…I just don't quite get it." He took a swallow of his wine. "We didn't really have a whole lot to talk about."

Lynne glanced pointedly at the kitchen clock.

Ethan grinned, now finally looking at least a little abashed. "Yeah, yeah. So we shot a few games of pool, and then watched the end of the Blazers game. I didn't realize it was this late."

"That's all right," Lynne said, not entirely convincingly.

Steph wiped down the counters and then said, "Lynne, I'm going to take off if you don't need anything else?"

"Oh, of course! Thank you for all your help." She came over and gave Steph a hug. "Don't get lost on your way home!"

Steph chuckled at their usual joke, and returned her line: "Don't worry, I promise to call you in the middle of the night if I do."

The porch light was on, but only minimal lights greeted her once she got inside the house. Steph set her purse and picnic basket down in the kitchen and went looking for David. He was curled up in their bed, clearly sound asleep.

Okay then. At least he was home. And not lost in his work. Or…the other stuff.

She closed the bedroom door softly and went back to the kitchen, putting the appetizer dishes away. Then she got a glass of water, taking it to her study and pulling out her laptop. Since her pie-tasting and talk with Lynne, she'd been thinking more and more about the idea of hosting group dinners for the community, and it was really appealing to her. Her initial instincts were still feeling right—she wanted the dinners to be for locals, not tourists; she didn't need to make any money on them, but wanted them to be as inclusive as possible.

The trouble she was having, as she researched the idea, was the venue. Orcas Island had lots of potential sites, and Lynne had given her a handful of contacts, but none of the places Steph had looked into made much sense for her particular project. She wanted a mostly-outdoor space, with the potential for shelter if the weather turned nasty, but everything that fit that bill was booked up years in advance. Also, many of those spaces were too large, and, though money was not a huge sticking point for her, costlier even than she had imagined.

She did know two separate people who had property with love-ly meadows on them that might be suitable, but a quick search of the county website revealed that the permitting process involved with even occasional, temporary meals-for-sale commerce was overwhelming. Not to mention the infrastructure: porta-potties, food preparers' handwashing stations, regulation food warmers and coolers…all the staff would be required to have Washington State food handlers' licenses…

And what if she bit the bullet and got all that taken care of, only to have Sam McLeod or someone like him decide that *her* business was the next one that needed quashing?

She could just make the meals free, take commerce out of it altogether, but Lynne had been right: people valued things that they paid for. Also, if she just wanted to feed the community, she could volunteer at the food bank, or one of the various churches.

She wanted…something just a little different than that. She wanted to forge a connection, to *create* a community. Like the Sunday Soup group, but bigger—but did they have to be forty or fifty people? If the dinners were small enough to be held at a large private home…

Hmm.

She stared into space for a long moment, thinking it through. Then she opened a Word doc on her laptop and started typing up notes, pouring out her thoughts in a long brainstorm.

Eventually, her thoughts wound down, and with them, her en-ergy. Time for bed. She closed the laptop, turned off the lights, and headed to the bedroom.

Chapter 8

ALICIA

On Monday, Alicia took the morning boat off-island to Anacortes. Usually she and Ron went off together, but he'd decided to stay home this time, saying he had too much to do.

She'd been deeply relieved and hadn't even gone through the motions of trying to talk him into coming with her. Last night had been unpleasant for both of them—more so even than usual, these days. It was like he had no patience whatsoever for her, and she felt much the same about him. It would do them good to get some space from each other, even just for a chunk of hours.

Maybe he actually was busy, too, who knew? He did spend rather a lot of time on his new writing project, whatever it was. He still wasn't talking to her about it, which was fine; let him have his process. Anyway, he never seemed all that impressed with her feedback anymore these days.

If he had ever been, and hadn't just been trying to be nice to her or something.

Ha! That was a good one. Ron Alderson being nice.

Alicia drove onto the MV Yakima; an orange-vested ferry worker directed her to park along the lower left-hand side lane. Once she was shoehorned into place, she got out of her car, squeezed past the other parked cars, and went upstairs to the passenger deck, where it was warm and light, and not even terribly crowded this time of year.

She bought a cup of coffee in the galley and took it to a seat by a west-facing window. *I will never tire of this view*, she thought. She sipped and gazed out at the passing islands, not pulling out the manuscript she'd brought along to work on, or even her phone. No sense mindlessly scrolling when there was all this to look at. It felt unbelievably good just to sit quietly, uninterrupted. She felt her whole body slowly begin to unclench.

All too soon, they were across the big water and pulling in to Anacortes. She threw away her empty coffee cup and headed back down to the car deck, ready to drive off.

Her first errand of the day, since the boat had been on time, was to drive an hour up to Bellingham. She and Ron hadn't been to Trader Joe's in months, and their shopping list had grown long. She even had things on her list from both Julie and Steph, who were excited that Alicia was willing to shop for them too.

"Of course," Alicia had said. "Why not?"

Once she got to the store, she remembered why not. Bellingham was just a bit south of the Canadian border, and the entire nation of Canada must not have a single Trader Joe's anywhere across its vast expanse, because it always seemed like the whole country was busy shopping in this very store. It was also the only TJ's anywhere north of Everett. The combination of Canadians and Western Washingtonians made this the most crowded TJ's Alicia had ever been in—and that included San Francisco's Masonic Avenue store, where the line of cars trying to get into the lot frequently stretched a block or more down Masonic itself. The city had actually created a new lane by removing parking on that section of the street.

Well, this was why she did this errand first. She pulled up her list on her phone, put her head down, and got methodically to work, muscling her way up one aisle and down the next until she'd covered the whole store.

By the end, her cart was piled high. She checked out, not bothering to separate her friends' groceries from her own—they could work it out later. Right now, she just wanted to get *out* of here.

Driving south on I-5, she checked the time. Weirdly, though it had seemed like a month or maybe a century, she had only been in there about forty-five minutes. She still had plenty of time to do Costco in Burlington as well.

Costco was more fun than TJ's, and *much* more fun without Ron. Alicia found the few items on her list, then slowly worked her way through the clothing department, hunting for the rare treasures amid the dross. Years ago, Costco had sold actual cashmere sweaters. Alas, those days were long gone, but you could usually find very decent athletic wear. She could use a new pair of pickleball leggings, and even another skort or two if they had them.

She found those things, plus a super cute floral blouse. She tossed those into her cart, then headed back for the grocery section. She hadn't brought an ice chest so she couldn't buy anything very perishable, but that was okay—fruit and veggies would keep fine.

Then she had fun walking slowly down the wine aisle, imagining Ron's reaction should she be so presumptuous as to choose something—anything—to bring home.

I remember when I had my own taste in wine, she thought, looking at all the pretty bottles. Okay, it wasn't a terribly *refined* taste; but she knew what she liked, and she could just…bring it home and drink it. Or not. There just wasn't all this angst about the whole thing.

Oh well.

She pushed her cart back to the front of the store and checked out, then loaded everything comfortably into the car.

And she *still* had enough time for a leisurely late lunch at her favorite Asian restaurant in Anacortes. She even ordered a hot sake, speaking of egregious, *have-you-no-palate-what-is-wrong-with-you* adult beverage selections.

As she sat alone at her table, sipping her sake, eating an eel-cucumber roll smothered in sauce, with a hamachi handroll and saba nigiri cued up on deck, she felt the oddest sensation. A lightness, a sense of airiness. It wasn't the alcohol from the sake, she was pretty sure; she felt as though she could almost float away. On soft, warm clouds.

It's peace, she thought, after a long moment's reflection. *I'm at peace*. It was like her unclenching on the ferry, except…deeper. More.

She took another sip of the sake and then savored the last piece of the eel-cucumber roll. Delicious.

Her final appointment of the day was the ostensible reason for the whole off-island excursion: a haircut. Yes, there were salons on Orcas—several of them, in fact, and they were perfectly good—but Alicia had been seeing Kendra since she'd moved to the island. So when Kendra moved from Orcas to Anacortes to be closer to her aging mother, Alicia had followed her.

When you found somebody who did this good a job with your hair, you didn't let them go.

Kendra grinned happily when Alicia walked in to the busy salon, waving from her station near the back. "Come on down!" she called.

Alicia walked past the six other chairs, all full of women in various stages of being beautified—folded foils, getting a blow-out, or just a bang trim. She settled into Kendra's chair and grinned at her in the mirror.

"Long time no see!" Kendra said. "How are things?"

"Things are fine, I guess," Alicia said. "Has it been longer than usual? I can't remember."

"Oh hon, I think it's been a while. Last fall maybe? Look how long your hair has gotten!" She picked up the ends of Alicia's hair and examined them critically. "You're lucky you've got so much body, but I see some split ends here." She dropped the ends and met Alicia's eyes in the mirror again. "So, what are we doing today? Same cut as usual?"

"I don't see why not—you can't improve on perfection."

Kendra laughed and waved a hand in dismissal. "If there's anything perfect here, it's your amazing hair. I just whack away at it and it falls into place like magic."

"If that were true, then anyone could cut it. I could cut it myself."

"Don't you dare." They laughed, and Kendra added, "Come on over to the sinks, let's get you shampooed."

Ah, the best part of the whole haircut. Alicia sank back into the chair and lost herself to the pleasure of it.

"So, what's new out on Orcas?" Kendra asked, once they were back at her station.

"Hmm, not a whole lot, I don't think. Your old salon seems to be limping along without you."

Kendra laughed. "Oh, I'm sure they're doing fine. Didn't they hire that hotshot young stylist from L.A.? How's she doing?"

"I wouldn't know—I never set foot in there, you know that."

"You are so loyal!"

"No, just smart," Alicia said. "A good hair stylist is worth her weight in gold."

They smiled at each other in the mirror as Kendra began trimming.

"Oh, I know what's new," Alicia added. "Have you heard about the Great Parking Meter Debacle?"

"No!" Kendra's eyes widened. "Parking meters? On Orcas?"

Alicia told her the whole story, as much as she understood it anyway. "I'm not nearly as involved as my friend Julie is, but there's this new commission or something, and they're talking about 'beautification' as well, so it probably won't stop with just parking meters."

"Jeez, that's awful—and sounds like just the opposite of beautiful to me." Kendra snipped and then measured the lengths on both sides of Alicia's part, making sure the ends were even. "What are they thinking? Orcas isn't *Seattle*."

"Exactly! That's what we all say."

"I don't even think we have parking meters out here in Anacortes."

Alicia thought about it. "No, you're right, you don't." She started to shake her head, but Kendra was performing some sort of delicate operation around her eyes, so she held still. "I don't know what the thinking is, but Julie's furious about it. She's even had a couple of run-ins with the guy organizing the whole thing."

Kendra chuckled. "I remember Julie—she has that store with the fancy handmade books, right?"

"That's her."

"She's great, but I wouldn't want to be on her bad side. She's powerful."

"Is she? I hadn't thought of her that way, but…I guess you're right. She knows what she wants and she isn't afraid to go get it."

"We should all be so mighty." Kendra gave her a sad smile. "That guy won't stand a chance."

"Gosh, I hope not," Alicia said. "So how are *you* doing? Seriously, enough about me."

"I'm not sure I heard anything about you specifically, hon, but fine, be that way." Kendra winked. "I'm all right. Mom takes up a lot of my off time, so I keep out of trouble."

"How is she doing?"

"She's pretty good, considering. She really wants to stay in her home, so I'm doing everything I can to help keep her there. It's a lot, but moving her—anywhere—would be even more work. So we're hanging in there."

"It's good of you to do that for her."

Kendra shrugged. "Well, it was good of her to bring me into this world and take care of me for twenty-odd years, so I guess this is my way of trying to even the score up a bit."

"Still. Not everyone would do what you're doing." She thought about her own parents—at least they had each other. They were so fiercely independent, they would likely never put up with Alicia trying to help them out, no matter how gently she tried to do it. Though who knew? Matt's dad had apparently been pretty independent until he literally couldn't live alone anymore. "Do you miss Orcas?"

"Deeply. But I have to say, it's awful convenient to be able to just get into my car and drive somewhere, without having to mess with the ferries."

"Tell me about it. No, actually, don't—I don't want to bring my mood down."

When Kendra blew Alicia's hair out, it looked fantastic, as always. "Thank you so much," Alicia told her.

"My pleasure, hon. Don't be such a stranger!"

"I won't," Alicia promised. "In fact let's get another appointment in the calendar before I leave."

They hugged at the door before Alicia left. Time to head to the ferry terminal, speaking of the devil.

As she sat in her car waiting for her boat to arrive, Alicia leaned back and closed her eyes. She could still smell the product that Kendra used—a scent Alicia loved, but she wouldn't buy it to use at home. It was the special scent of Haircut Day, and it somehow seemed even more special than usual today.

Was it just because it had been so long? Was it because she'd been away all day, doing her own thing (even if that thing was just shopping and lunch and a haircut), without anyone all up in her business…without *Ron* all up in her business?

He's a lot of work, she thought. *I love him, I love our life together, but oh, he's a lot of work sometimes.*

She sighed, and pulled out her phone to check the ferry app. Her boat was about fifteen minutes late—not terrible, in the grand scheme of things.

She put her phone away and rummaged around the back seat

for her satchel. Might as well work on that manuscript.

STEPH

TUESDAY WAS ONE of David's work-at-home days, as Steph now knew from the shared calendar he'd promised to keep updated with such information. He was of course already up and in his office when she awoke. She prepared a small bagel-based breakfast, made him a cup of sweetened tea just how he liked it, and carried his plate and cup down the hall, tapping on his office door before easing it open.

He turned around as she walked in, looking startled. She lifted the plate and cup to show him it was only her with breakfast, not a zombie attack, then set them on the corner of his desk, far from his keyboard and note papers. She tried not to look at any of the papers, though he didn't seem concerned. He just gave her a small smile as he returned his eyes to the screen. His fingers had never stopped moving on the keyboard.

In the early afternoon, when he logged out of his day job, he emerged from his office and headed to the fridge, as he usually did. *"Share as much of your life with him as possible...your hopes and dreams,"* Julie had advised, so Steph was waiting for him, with a nice light lunch prepared. "Join me?" she asked, nodding toward the kitchen table.

"Oh, thanks," he said, seeming distracted. "I'm not that hungry, I was just going to get something to drink."

"Okay, but do you have a minute to talk? I want to run something by you."

"Um, sure." He sat at the table without getting himself anything to drink.

Steph served herself some salad. "Are you sure you don't want any of this?"

"Maybe a little."

She dished some onto his plate. He took a bite. "It's good."

"Thanks." She smiled, and took a bite of her own. It was indeed good—sort of a riff on Cobb salad, but with only the yummy things. Steph was never a fan of hard-boiled eggs in salads. They looked pretty in the pictures, but they never behaved out here in the real world. Anyway, the obvious correct way to eat both boiled eggs and salad was *egg salad*. "Remember how I told you a while back about Lynne's idea that I should do community dinners and charge people for them?"

He frowned. "Maybe? I thought you didn't want to go into the catering or restaurant business."

"I don't, and this isn't that. Remember the Red Rabbit Farm dinners?" He nodded. "This would be more like that, but probably even a bit smaller. I'm pretty sure I mentioned this?" She was entirely sure she had, but, okay.

"I don't know. I don't remember." He pushed his salad around on his plate, but then took another bite.

"It doesn't matter. Well, I've been thinking more about it, and doing some research, and I think it could work. Except I've been having a tough time figuring out a venue. This would need to be in the summertimes or at least the late spring through early fall, because they should be outdoors, and obviously when the weather is pleasant—but all the venues are totally booked up during the good weather, of course."

He nodded again.

"So the other night I had an idea…our back yard is large and comfortable—plenty of room to set up a couple of tables, enough to feed up to maybe twenty people. And the bigger greenhouse has that nice open space in the middle, where we could move inside if it got cold or started to rain or something. Or we could serve from there, in any case. We have all these bathrooms; we wouldn't need to get porta-potties; and my kitchen is more than good enough to cook for such a crowd. I'll have to get it certified by the county as a cottage kitchen, but I read over the requirements and it's got all it needs." Thank goodness for her insistence on separate sink areas when they'd remodeled! She'd just thought about her own convenience, not commercial kitchen regulations, but it would have been one of the most difficult requirements if she'd needed to retrofit. "I'd want to start with maybe one or two the first year and see how it goes, but I'm really excited and I think it—"

"You want to have these events *here?*"

She blinked, caught off stride. "Yes, that's what I'm saying. Just a few at first—or we can talk about it after the first one…" She stopped, seeing his face. "I know this isn't your thing, but what's the matter?"

"I just…it just seems like a lot of people, here, at the house. *In* the house. That's all." He looked so uncomfortable—no, not just that, but frightened almost.

"David. Honey." She kept her voice gentle, trying to mask her surprise. "I'm not pushing back, but I would like to understand. I host soup groups here, and neighborhood association meetings, and parties like the Christmas party." He was nodding, looking miserable. "I get that this is a little different, that these would be people we don't necessarily know—strangers. Is that the problem?"

He shrugged. "Maybe. I don't know. It feels…different."

She watched his face. "I would be charging them, but I don't know if I mentioned, I'm going to limit the attendance to locals. I don't want to go into the business of courting the tourist trade. Not that there's anything wrong with that—a big part of the island's economy is dependent on tourism—but I'm more interested in building community. My dream is that the same people come again and again; that it becomes something like our Christmas party, but outdoors. After a few times, they wouldn't be strangers. And you wouldn't ever need to attend them if you didn't want to, though of course you would always be welcome."

"Are you sure there's no other place you can do it?"

"I can keep looking, and asking around, but I did kind of hit a dead end." She could talk to her friends with meadows…but this was a pretty big ask. Guests would have to use their houses, at least for the bathrooms, unless they wanted to have porta-potties on their land. And this was not to mention Steph's use of their kitchens—assuming they could be made compliant with the regulations.

"Thank you." He leaned back in his chair, sort of folding in on himself. But he did take another bite of salad.

"Will you do me a favor, though?" she asked. At his nod, she said, "Will you think about it? It's obvious something is bothering you about this idea, but I'm just not quite sure what it is—and I'm not convinced you know either."

He shrugged. "I just…" He looked away, then sighed and looked back at her. "I don't know."

She gazed at him, wishing she could peer into his mind. "Well, I'd love to talk more about it if and when you have more thoughts."

"Okay."

"I promise not to just bull on ahead if you really don't want me to do it here," she went on.

"Okay. Thank you." He gave her a watery smile. "So, um, I'm really tired. I think I might take a nap."

"All right."

He pushed back from the table and picked up his plate. She was happy to see that he'd eaten all his lunch, at least. He carried his plate to the sink and headed down the hall to their bedroom, closing the door behind him.

Well, that was a big old step in the wrong direction, Steph thought as she cleaned up the dishes. Of course she hadn't expected him to be excited about the idea of her hosting these dinners at their house, but he knew how important being social, and particularly entertaining, was to her, and he'd always been okay with it in the past—floating around the edges of a gathering if he was feeling up to it, or being scarce if he needed to.

He so rarely just said no to her. Which, despite his not using that exact word today, was essentially what had happened here.

Was that okay, though? Shouldn't he be able to say no to her? Steph really, truly didn't want to bully him—god no. That's what everyone else in his life did. If he really felt strongly about this, then she would find another way to make these events happen.

Or just give up the idea. Her life was full enough, wasn't it?

You're bored, Lynne had told her, and Steph kept hearing those words. If they weren't true, they wouldn't be rolling around in her mind on repeat like this.

She had been so excited when this idea had taken hold, envisioning herself as some sort of Orcas Island Barefoot Contessa, comfortably feeding big groups of happy, interesting people. Like a rural salon. Mixing and matching, guiding her guest lists—and, yes, she could admit it, bringing in a little income.

It was nice not to have to work a dull, soul-sucking job. But wouldn't it be even nicer to have remunerative work that was meaningful and fulfilling?

She dried her hands and started to head to her study, but turned and instead went out into the back garden. It was still early March, so most everything was dormant, if not entirely dead. Even the greenhouses were not doing much, and smelled a little mildewy. Soon it would be time to start seeds, and then to buy little starter pots of annuals at the island's wonderful new nursery.

She tried to envision the yard with a long table of diners. Of course they'd had parties out here in summers past, but not with sit-down meals. She would want to get several long farm-style tables, probably; rustic wood, something like that. Put them end to end, running straight through the middle of the open part of the yard, stretching between the two greenhouses. Italian party lights strung overhead. She paced it out, measuring the space. Twenty or twenty-two people could fit in here easily.

It would be *so much fun*.

Steph shook off the image and went back inside. Their bedroom door was still closed; David didn't nap very often, but when he did, he tended to take rather long naps.

Was this thing with his parents and their company sending him back into an actual depressive episode? How long should she wait to ask him more directly about that?

Well, at least long enough to try to successfully follow Julie's advice. Steph would sure as heck not be bringing up any more difficult topics today. The look of fear on his face when he asked if she wanted to have the events here stayed with her.

At dinner, he still looked sad and tired, though (thankfully) not quite so frightened. "Did you have a nice nap?" she asked him.

"It was fine." He looked at her mournfully. "Sorry I'm such a drag lately."

"That's okay," she said, feeling something small but vital relax in her. Was this an opening? "I just wondered…you don't seem quite yourself these days. Is something bothering you?" *I miss our snuggles before the fire in the evenings*, she thought about adding, but didn't want to push it.

"No, not really. I'm just tired, and feeling…I don't know." He pushed his fork at his food, eyes down at his plate, though not lifting a bite to his mouth. Then he looked up at her. "You should just divorce me and go live the big, busy, full, happy life you deserve."

She reached across the table and took his hand. "You can tell me that as many times as you like, but I'm not going anywhere. Unless *you* want a divorce?"

His blue eyes widened and he shook his head vigorously. "No. I love you."

"Well, I love you too, you silly man. So no more talk of divorce."

He gave her a small, fragile smile. "This is good," he said, finally taking another bite.

"Thank you."

MATT

JUST WHEN MATT was about to make another doctor's appointment for Gordon to see if they could get to the bottom of whatever was going on, he mellowed out, with as little apparent outside cause as there had been for his sliding into the difficult phase. He became more cheerful, amenable to small walks around the house and garden, even to drinking water (though he still preferred sweet juices or sodas).

Maybe he was using the full-spectrum light on the sly, and didn't want to admit it to Matt, after fighting it so hard? Though Matt didn't think so; Gordon didn't have a lot of "sly" left in him these days, despite what he might think.

They were sitting in the living room playing a game of Crazy 8's when Megan texted. *You still up?*

Matt picked up his phone and typed back to her. *Yes, playing cards with Dad.*

Oh—sorry to interrupt.

Not a problem. Do you want to talk? We'll probably be through here in about fifteen minutes.

Sure, she wrote back. *That would be great.*

"Sorry," he said to his dad, playing a card. "Your turn."

"Who was that?" Gordon asked, with a smile.

"Megan, Julie's daughter. Remember her? She lives in Portland?"

Gordon nodded, though his eyes were vague. "I like Julie."

"You like Megan too, and her sister Lori. Remember Steph's Christmas party? They were the two young women who sat with us in the kitchen."

"Oh yes! Such pretty girls!"

"Yes, and nice, too. So, go ahead and play a card if you can—it's your turn."

"Are we in a rush?" Gordon asked, with a wink.

Matt nodded. "We are, because I'm going to call Megan as

soon as we're done here and I get you off to bed."

"Ha!" Gordon laughed, and played.

Once his dad was comfortably tucked in for the night, Matt settled back in the living room with a short glass of scotch over ice. He'd still not completely regained his taste for whiskey after his overindulgence right after Heather left, but it was coming back. Thank goodness.

He took a sip and called Megan.

"Hey," she said. "How's it going up there?"

"Pretty good, actually." He told her about his dad's new agreeableness. "It's probably just another phase, of course, but I'll take it."

"Absolutely," she agreed. "One day at a time. That gets you through the hard times *and* lets you appreciate the good things when they happen."

"Yeah." He smiled, though she couldn't see him; it was only a voice call. "How are things down there?"

She huffed out a little sigh. "Things are fine here, but I wanted to ask you about my mom, if you've seen her recently."

Matt sat up a little in his chair, alerted by something in her tone. "We had soup group on Sunday; Gavin came too. What do you want to know?"

"I'm not worried about Gavin—they're clearly perfect together. But every time I talk to her, she goes on and on about this parking meter thing. It's starting to sound a little obsessive, you know?"

"Well, it's important to her," Matt said, scrambling to think. "What has she told you about it?"

"Oh, just how dumb the whole thing is. I know she's mad that the measure passed, but, come on, what's the big deal?"

Had Julie not told Megan the latest? It was entirely possible—maybe she didn't want to worry her daughters. "I'm sure she sees it as a threat to her business," Matt hedged, hoping Megan would say more.

"That's silly. People aren't going to stop visiting Orcas Island because they'll have to pay a few bucks to park. She needs to get over this. I mean, it's not even her issue."

Clearly Julie *hadn't* told Megan about the inspection letter and the confrontation with McLeod. Matt was absolutely not going to spill those beans—but he was going to tell Julie about this phone conversation. "Actually, it is her issue," he managed. "The county dug up the sidewalk right in front of her store not once but twice, and the guy behind the commission had her car towed. This is personal. Also, she worked really hard fighting the measure—she put a lot of energy into that. Of course she's disappointed at how it turned out."

"But that's just it: the thing passed, it's a done deal. Can't she just set it down and move on?"

"It hasn't been that long since the measure passed," Matt said. "Does she really keep bringing it up every time you talk to her?" And if so, why, if she wasn't going to tell Megan what was really going on? *Ugh, I do not like being in the middle here,* Matt thought.

"Well not *every* time—I may have exaggerated a teensy bit—but, I don't know, she just still seems a little too upset about it."

"I'm sure it touched a nerve," Matt said. "She cares about this island—we all do, but she runs a business right in the heart of it, a business that depends on its being easy to find and walk into. And, you know, she's not independently wealthy or anything, so if something comes along that threatens that business—"

"Right, you're right," Megan said with another sigh. "It's an existential threat, even if it seems like a pretty minor issue to the rest of us." She chuckled. "Am I too impatient? You can be honest with me, dude; I've been told before that I can tend to run away with things. That I'm too much of an analytical thinker and don't let people have their emotions."

"I don't know," Matt said softly. "You seem perfectly empathetic to me." *You seem perfect to me.* "But I'll give her a call soon and see how she's doing."

"I'm sure she's fine. It's actually helpful just to talk it over." Megan laughed again. "And with someone who isn't Lori, before you ask."

"Oh?"

"Yeah. I talked to her about this, and she was all, 'We should go up and see her right away!'"

Matt's heart leapt. *Yes, come up here right away!* "Well, is that the world's worst idea?" he asked, carefully.

Her laughter bubbled over now. "Yes, it is, actually; it's grant writing season, and we were just up there for a super long visit at Christmas. We are planning to come up for Lynne's big art opening in May."

"That will be nice. It'll be great to see you again."

"And I am looking forward to seeing you again," she said, seriously. "My friend."

"My friend," he echoed.

They ended their call soon after that; it was getting late, and there wasn't much more to say.

Except for all the things they'd agreed not to say to each other.

Chapter 9

JULIE

"This is the worst part of the evening," Gavin murmured sleepily. "Zero stars, do not recommend."

Julie turned and smiled down at him in the bed as she continued getting dressed after their lovely dinner and even lovelier after-dinner entertainment. She agreed with him, of course, but she would still rather drive home tonight than have to scramble to get up and ready and into town in time to open her shop tomorrow morning. "You know if I stayed over, you'd just try to, ahem, *delay* my departure."

He grinned up at her. It was a wicked grin, and it was a gorgeous grin, and it almost delayed her right then and there. "I'll have to get to work too, you know."

"So you say." In the past, they had bantered about moving in together, both knowing that they valued their own spaces too much to actually do so, at least for the time being. But the threat of having to give up her adorable cottage was too painful to joke about right now. Julie could see living together someday...but she did not want to be forced into the decision.

She buttoned her blouse, then leaned down and gave him a long slow kiss, staying just out of reach of his hands which were all too ready to drag her back down into the bed. Once she eased free of the kiss, she added, "I'll see you tomorrow—are you still staying at my place? After book group?"

"Yes, if you'll have me."

She gave him a saucy grin. "It would be my great pleasure to have you." She sat on the edge of the bed and pulled her socks on. "Funny, I never imagined being in a long-distance relationship at my age."

Gavin snorted with laughter. "I don't know which part of that sentence is silliest. Were you ever in a long-distance relationship?"

"No, I guess I wasn't. And I can see why not: this whole saying-goodbye thing is for the birds."

She'd been sleeping over at his place on many of the nights when she didn't have to get up to open the shop the next day. These nights were suddenly fewer than they'd been, now that she'd taken her shop off its winter hours and back to a Tuesday-through-Sunday schedule. Staying here had been really nice. His house was charming, and his acreage was beautiful and peaceful. It would only get lovelier as spring and summer approached and his garden returned from dormancy.

Ugh: summer, when her shop would be open seven days a week. That had never seemed like a hardship, before she'd had somewhere else where she liked spending the nights. It had been enough to work hard every day, collapse exhausted into bed at night, and get up and do it all over again, secure in the knowledge that she was putting aside a good nest egg to carry her through the quieter seasons.

Now, a small part of her wished every month could be January, when the shop was entirely closed. This January had been an especially dreamy time, not just because of all the freedom to spend time with Gavin, but also all the creative work she'd gotten done. Not to mention it had been before the resurrected crisis with Mr. Vacation Rental Developer Sam McLeod.

Ah, such days of innocence.

I'm too young to retire, she thought, as she kissed Gavin one more time before getting her bag and slipping out into the night. *And I am in no way letting McLeod kick me out of my home. But someday...under my own terms...*

She let her mind wander as she made the drive back to town on the darkened roads. Of course retirement was tempting, especially if their sweet little town was going to be besmirched with greedy developers and their cronies. Still-mysterious cronies, at that; even Leslie, with her multi-generational local knowledge and pull, had so far been unable to find out any of the names of the so-called "working group." It probably didn't even exist.

Once McLeod's totally bogus inspection process was done and he'd managed to kick out Julie and anyone else he deemed unworthy of the commission's approval, what was he going to do next? Change the town's zoning laws to allow skyscrapers? Chain stores? Multi-story parking structures? *Stoplights?*

She shuddered at the very thought. There were no stoplights in all of San Juan County—not even in Friday Harbor, the county seat over on San Juan Island. And everyone who actually cared about the place liked it that way, thank you very much.

Why did newcomers always want to show up and ruin everything?

She had to roll her eyes at herself, privately. She'd been a newcomer, not even ten years ago. And she had changed some things, there was no denying that. Both the shop building and her cottage had been pretty run-down—which had been why she could afford them in the first place. She'd put a lot of sweat equity into both buildings since then, making them the charming places they were now: removing dump-loads of junk, adding bigger windows to the front of the shop, remodeling the tiny kitchen in her cottage to make it actually functional. She'd sanded and refinished the hardwood floors in both buildings her second year here—by herself, by hand. In her third year, she'd painted the shop; in her fourth, it had gotten its new roof.

But these were improvements, making her little part of the

island nicer and more functional—*actual* beautification, not
whatever McLeod thought he was doing. Did he really believe
his proposals were going to improve the landscape, or was he
just—somehow, she still had no idea exactly how—looking to
line his pockets? He couldn't possibly think parking meters were
beautiful.

Then again, who really knew how wealthy developers saw the
world? Maybe anything designed to take in money—selling a
previously free public resource, at that—was lovely to him.

Did he own a company that built or sold parking meters? Ooh,
if he did, and she could prove a conflict of interest...

But no. He would have been smarter than that; there would be
no trail that could lead back to him.

By now she was nearly to town, and feeling the sleepiness starting to settle on her. She'd stayed a bit later than she'd meant to
at Gavin's this evening; they'd just been feeling so comfortable
together, so easy. It would be nice to live with him someday, she
thought.

She'd never imagined getting married again—she hadn't even
envisioned living with a man again—but lately the idea didn't
seem all that bad.

THURSDAY EVENING AS soon as she closed the shop, Julie stopped
by her house to feed Fergie, and then continued on over to the
library.

Gavin met her at the front desk. "I've just ordered the pizzas—a veggie and a meat combo. They should be ready to pick
up in twenty minutes."

"Oh good. Do you think two will be enough?"

"We've got seven people confirmed, counting you and me."

She thought about it. "Yeah, two large pizzas should be enough.
I hope."

They walked together back to the meeting room. Gavin had
already bought the drinks—waters, sodas, and a bottle of red

wine. "I hope this one is okay?" he asked.

"Looks good to me. In fact, let's open it." She grinned at him. "Got to let it breathe, you know."

"You're the expert."

"Nah, just thirsty. And ready." She found a corkscrew near the little sink in the corner and opened the bottle, pouring a small measure into a plastic cup and taking a sip. "Yeah, this is fine. Too bad we don't have real wine glasses, though. I guess that's one benefit of having meetings at someone's house."

"Maybe one of the book group members will offer their house." He glanced at his watch. "I should probably leave to get the pizzas—do you want to walk down with me, or wait here?"

"I should probably stay here in case someone comes early." The meeting didn't start till seven, but Julie had learned over the years that the concept of "island time" didn't always mean people arrived late to things…sometimes it meant they showed up fifteen or more minutes early. "Do you know everyone who's signed up to come?"

"I've met everyone, but the only person I really know is Will."

"Well, this should be fun, getting to know new people," Julie told him. "Anyway—you go, I'll hold down the fort here."

He kissed her and set out.

Julie took her plastic cup of wine to the table, trying to decide if she should sit at the head, or just near the head. She supposed she was technically in charge, though she hoped that in time, the group would coalesce and not really need a leader—like the soup group.

For now, she sat at the head of the table.

She took the book out of her bag and started thumbing through it, just to have something to do with her hands (besides drinking wine). She didn't have to refresh her memory of the book—it was, as Gavin had promised, her favorite one of Libby Perrine's, *The Glory*, one she had reread many times.

Which hadn't stopped her from rereading it again last week,

just because she could. She did always see new things in it, new layers, new nuances. What an amazing author Libby Perrine was. It was going to be wonderful to discuss this book with others.

Despite herself, she had gotten caught up in reading the scene where Jacob takes Claire to meet his parents for the first time, and was startled when the meeting room door opened. Gavin walked in with two pizza boxes, returning Julie to the here-and-now. "Oh wow, those smell good," she said, as he set them in the middle of the table.

"No one else is here yet?" he asked, as though someone might be hiding under the table.

"Nope."

He eyed the fragrant boxes. "Should we eat now, or wait for the others?"

She looked at her watch. One minute till seven. "I guess we could wait till the official starting time, anyway. We don't want to seem rude."

"We don't want cold pizzas either," Gavin pointed out.

"Well, yeah. There's a time and a place for cold pizza, and that is *not* when there are fresh hot pizzas in front of us."

"Exactly." He got himself a soda out of the ice chest by the sink and sat down at Julie's left. Seeing the book, he said, "Oh rats, I left my copy at home."

"That's okay. You can use mine if you want to look at something specific."

He smiled at her and glanced up at the big clock on the wall. Two minutes after seven.

She sipped her wine.

At five after, Gavin said, "Okay, I think we can safely eat some pizza without seeming hasty."

"Thank god," she said, reaching out and pulling one of the boxes toward her. It was the meat combo; she pulled out a still-steaming slice and took a big bite. "Wow that's good."

"Yeah." Gavin took one as well. "Ooh, I forgot napkins, hang on." He got up and set his slice on top of the pizza box.

"Don't leave that there!"

He picked it back up again and looked around. "Well I'm not going to put it on the table."

"Just eat it—get napkins afterward."

"Yes ma'am."

They grinned at each other and ate their slices. "All right, may I go find us some napkins now please?" he asked, with exaggerated politeness.

"Yes you may."

He rummaged around by the sink, then left the room, returning a minute later with a handful of paper towels and a stack of paper plates. "Look what I found!"

"Ah, that's even more civilized," Julie said, as he handed her one. She took a slice of the veggie pizza so that the plate wouldn't feel lonely. Gavin did the same.

At ten after, they'd each finished two slices of pizza. Julie refilled her wine.

At quarter after, Julie asked, "It was supposed to be tonight, wasn't it?"

"Yes. Yes it was." He sipped his soda. "I sent email reminders this afternoon. I even got a couple confirmations."

His phone dinged with a text; he pulled it out of his pocket and looked at it. "It's Will. He can't make it after all—he had an emergency come up at his house in Arizona that he has to go deal with."

"So he's leaving *tonight*?" she asked. "Right now?"

Gavin shrugged. "That's what he said." He showed her his phone. Yep, that's what he said.

"Huh. Well that leaves four other people unaccounted for. Did you get phone numbers from them? We could try texting."

"No, just their email addresses, on the signup sheet," Gavin said.

"Huh," she said, again.

At twenty after seven, Julie reached for another slice of meat pizza. Gavin said, "Might as well," and took another slice of veggie.

At seven thirty, she said, "Should we try emailing everyone? But that's dumb," she answered herself. "We should have gotten phone numbers. Or at least given everyone *our* numbers so they could let us know if they couldn't make it."

"We'll do that next time," Gavin promised. "I didn't even think about it."

"Next time."

At seven forty, there was a flash of movement outside the glass door. Both Gavin and Julie sat up, eager, but it was just someone walking past.

At seven forty-five, another library employee poked her head in. "How's it going? Oh," she said, seeing the two of them, and all the uneaten pizza. "No one came?"

"Apparently," Julie said, trying not to sound testy.

"There might have been a mix-up," Gavin said, though she knew that he knew there hadn't been.

"Gosh. Sorry," the employee said, and ducked back out again.

"Do you want a piece of pizza?" Gavin called after her.

"No thanks!" she yell-whispered back, in that way known only to librarians.

At seven fifty, Julie said, "Well, I don't think anyone's coming, and I'm full. I guess we could talk about the book ourselves." She smiled at him. "Did you just love it? I so enjoyed reading it again. She's a genius."

"Ah. Well." Gavin gave her an uncomfortable smile.

"It's okay if you didn't like it!" she rushed to assure him. "I know she's not for everyone—it was sweet of you to even give it a try."

"Um." His smile grew more strained. "I, uh, actually, didn't quite finish the book."

"Oh that's fine too! I know you're busy. How far did you get?"

"Er. I." She could see him cringe, visibly shrinking down in his chair. "Didn't quite make it through the first chapter, actually…"

"What?"

"I thought there'd be more time! The days got away from me, and…well, I also thought there'd be more people here! That you might not even notice…that I could pick up the gist of the story from the discussion, and…you know, sort of sneak along that way…"

"Gavin!" Julie wailed in frustration.

"And I didn't want to disappoint you!" he said. "And see, I did anyway!"

"Oh, for crying out loud…" She felt like she wanted to cry, and also laugh. It was just too ridiculous. So she did a little of both, knuckling tears off her face as she hiccupped and sniffled and chuckled. "I'm doomed to never have a book group, aren't I?"

"Not at all," he said, reaching up and gently wiping away a tear. "I promise, we will regroup, we will make this work. This is my grand romantic gesture to win you back, after all. If it's doomed, it means that *we're* doomed, and I won't have that."

Now she was fully laughing. "Gavin Jones, you wonderful lunatic."

"Julie Pessel, my beloved bibliophile."

And they kissed amid the paper plates, grease-stained napkins, and cold pizza.

STEPH

IT WAS LATE morning on Pi Day—her turn for soup group, featuring savory pies along with her soup offering—and Steph was not even close to ready. She hadn't been to the grocery store yet, so she couldn't finalize the menu. She'd gone looking for scallops in the chest freezer and hadn't found them, though her database showed that there should still be three packages. She'd dithered about the soup itself so much, trying to come up with something that would stand up to the pies, that nothing sounded good anymore.

Ordinarily, she could pull off a dinner party for six or seven people in her sleep. But she was distracted and worried about David, and unsure what to do next.

On Friday evening, he had worked late at his office in town. Steph had told herself that she didn't really expect he'd come home for a "date night," given the way things had been going, but she'd been disappointed all the same. When he finally did get home, he had been withdrawn and quiet. And not hungry. And tired. And apologetic, when he realized it was Friday night. She felt certain he wasn't intending to hurt her, but it hurt all the same.

Her program of trying to soft-pedal this, to draw him gently back toward her rather than confront him directly, hadn't failed, but it hadn't succeeded either. It had fallen right in the middle, effectively immobilizing her. David would spend a day or two being more loving and present, so she'd think they were getting somewhere, only for him to shift back to being remote and morose. But just when she would decide it was time to speak with him about this, he'd relax and engage with her again. They'd even had some snuggle-evenings before the fire.

Yesterday, he'd offered to atone for missing Friday's dinner by helping her with the preparations for tonight's gathering; she'd thanked him but told him she could handle it fine. He did know his way around the kitchen, and they used to cook together from time to time, but the ugly little truth was that if he were going to feel like he owed her something, she would rather have him show up for the dinner than its preparation.

Though he would most likely do neither. Part of her wished she could cancel tonight. Of course, the group would understand if she needed to, but…she'd really rather not.

Steph stood at the kitchen island, where she had been staring down at an open cookbook without seeing it for some time now. It had been so wonderful, their breakthrough, their renewed intimacy. She had been filled with hope and joy, with the delight of having a true partner again. They had spent the last few years quietly drifting into separate lives without actually meaning to. How naïve of her to have believed that all she had had to do was speak up about it, and everything had gotten repaired.

Did he even want to be her partner, her husband? Or was he just such a people-pleaser—a *Steph*-pleaser—that he had pushed himself beyond his limits trying to make her happy, suppressing his own wants and needs? Was this why he was hiding whatever was going on with his parents from her?

God, she hoped not; she hoped he truly wanted to share his life with her, all the way. He had seemed happy when they'd reconnected—as happy as she had been, maybe even more. She thought back to that first date-night dinner: him in his wedding suit, stealthily arranging flowers on the dining room table. A lump grew in her throat as tears stung her eyes.

We can't go back to the way we were. I can't go back to that.

She had been living her life half-asleep. It was so clear now. She'd been coexisting, however comfortably it might have seemed, with a man who was basically a roommate; puttering around the house; seeing the same small group of friends. Dear friends, of course, and a great house on a lovely island, and all the rest; but she had been running in place for so long, she hadn't even understood she was going nowhere.

Now that she'd woken up, had gotten excited about a big new endeavor—community dinners—and a rekindled romantic partnership with David, she could not put herself back into the tiny box she'd been living in. She wouldn't fit anymore...and she didn't want to.

I need to talk to him. She'd given the gentle approach enough time; if it were going to work, it would have by now. She glanced at the clock. *After I get through this dinner party.*

For now, she really needed to do the shopping, or there wouldn't *be* a dinner party.

She closed the cookbook and pulled up her grocery list app on her phone, making decisions. The simpler soup would be fine; she'd been overthinking this. Eventually, she tucked her phone back into her pocket and walked down the hallway to his office door.

"Just a minute," he called, after she knocked. Then, "What is it?"

"I'm heading to the grocery store. I should be back in about an hour and a half."

The door opened. David looked drawn, pale. "Do you want me to come with you?"

"Do you want to come?"

He shifted his weight. "I really would like to help, if I can."

Oh, you're breaking my heart, my love, she thought. "Sure. Are you ready to go now?"

"Give me five minutes."

He met her in the front hall, looking fresher. He'd changed his shirt, combed his hair, and maybe splashed water on his face. "Do you want me to drive?" he asked.

"If you like."

He pushed the garage-door button beside the front door. "I'd be happy to."

As she climbed into the passenger seat of his Audi, she tried to remember how long it had been since she'd been in this car, while at the same time marveling at how clean he kept it. Her car was always a jumble of half-empty water bottles, receipts, trash, reusable grocery bags—"Oops," she said, as he was backing out of the garage.

He braked. "What is it?"

"Forgot the grocery bags." She flashed him an apologetic smile. "I'll just grab them out of my car."

Eventually, they were on the road to Eastsound. It was the ideal venue for a conversation, she thought: stuck in the car together. Yet it was a terrible place for any conversation that was serious and emotional. *I'm tired of chatting, though*, she thought.

So it was David who broke the silence.

"Not to keep flogging a dead horse," he said, "but I want you to know that I truly am sorry about how I've been lately. I really didn't mean to miss Friday dinner."

"I forgive you," she said. "And thank you."

"Yeah." He sighed. "I did not intend to break my promise to you. I'll make a better effort—and you can feel free to text me if I lose track of time again."

"I don't want to be a nag. I want you to *want* to spend time with me."

"I do!" he said, turning to glance at her. "I really do, Steph. I just…I'm working on my stuff, but…it's hard."

"I know it is," she said gently. "I…don't really know what to do here, to be honest."

"You're doing it. Just be yourself." He shrugged.

"I can't really be anyone else," she said, trying for a light tone but not quite hitting it. "I wish I could help you, she added.

"You can't fix me," he said. "I don't know if anyone can."

She studied his face as he watched the road. His blue eyes were alert; she could see the small tension in his jaw. "Do you want to try a new therapist? Or a different medication?"

"No," he said, too quickly. He must have heard himself; he flashed her an apologetic smile. "I mean, I don't think I want to make such a big change right now. But we can keep talking about it, if you want."

"That's fair," Steph said. "We don't need to figure any of this out today—especially when I have a dinner party to put together."

"And if you really don't need me to help with that, I'll stay out of your way," he said, signaling to turn into Eastsound.

"I'm happy for the shopping help," she said.

Which was indeed true: they divided up the list and met back at the cashiers in near-record time. David bagged up the groceries while Steph paid.

On the drive back home, he said, "I don't deserve you."

"What?"

"You're just…unbelievably patient. I'm not worth it."

"I told you last week not to go there," Steph said. "You are absolutely worth it. You deserve me, and I deserve you, and we *both* deserve to be happy together. Okay?"

"Okay," he said, after a minute. He glanced over at her. "Okay, and thank you."

"You are so welcome. I love you, David."

"I love you, Steph."

This will be a good opening for tomorrow's talk, she thought.

Once they got home, he helped her unload the groceries, then said, "I think I'll take a nap."

"Sounds good." Maybe if he were more rested, he'd at least show up for part of the evening.

She got going on the dinner, setting up the ingredients in the different areas of the kitchen for maximum efficiency. At the pastry station (a deep built-in marble surface, at a lower height than the regular countertops, with all the flours and sugars and other baking supplies in cabinets just above it), three stiff lumps of dough from the freezer waited to be rolled out, but she'd gotten bogged down with all the chopping and slicing for her ginger lemongrass Tom Kha Gai soup. So much for simple!

By the time the soup base was simmering on the stove, she had at last fallen into a rhythm, her mind and body working together to do the thing she loved *almost* best in the world: working to feed a small crowd.

As she rolled out the dough for the first pie, the doorbell rang. *Huh*, she thought, looking up at the kitchen clock. Way too early for any of the guests to be arriving. She set the rolling pin down, wiped her hands, and pulled her phone out of her pocket, just in case she'd missed a text or call, but there was nothing.

So she headed out to answer the door.

The bell rang again before she reached it. "I'm coming!" she called out, opening it as the chimes stilled.

A woman, a stranger, stood on her front porch. She was in her well-preserved seventies, Steph judged: ice-blond hair, clearly expensively maintained; skin that showed evidence of both youthful sun-worshiping and middle-aged plastic surgery (along with high-end cosmetics); sharp yet elegant cheekbones; and… sky-blue eyes that were unnervingly familiar. She wore a bland, casual-elegant outfit that probably cost more than Steph's BMW, and carried a tiny handbag that might be worth more than this house.

"You must be Stephanie," the woman said, looking her up and down with a strong air of judgment. "I'm looking for my son. David Palmer."

Steph's mouth fell open as her mind reeled. Then there were soft footsteps behind her, and David was at her back. She whirled to look at him. His eyes were still sleepy from his nap, but the rest of his face was a mask, letting absolutely nothing out. He grabbed Steph's hand, gripping it as though only she could save him.

That was all she needed to know. She turned back to the apparition on her doorstep and said, "I'm afraid this isn't a good time for us, so I'm just going to ask you to leave now." She gave her a sorry-not-sorry smile and started to close the door.

David's mother stepped forward, placing a pale-blue patent leather toe just on the threshold, silently daring Steph to crush it with the door.

Okay, you win that round, Steph thought, but didn't open the door any wider. She just stared back at the woman. *Now what?*

The woman narrowed her eyes and drew herself up to her full height, which was still a few inches shorter than Steph, though you'd never know it from the iron strength in her gaze. "I have gone to a considerable amount of trouble to come from a considerable distance away, to speak to my son. I would think at least he would have the courage to send me away himself, not to hide behind the skirts of his…woman."

David squeezed Steph's hand harder, but he cleared his throat. Steph turned to him again. He gave her the slightest nod, and looked at his mother. "I believe," he said, utterly without warmth, "that *my wife* has made our position quite clear. Please leave."

Probably only Steph could hear the tremor in his voice.

Or perhaps his mother could as well, for the faintest hint of a sly smile curved her elegant lips. The smile did not reach her eyes. "You have not seen me in three decades, and you are not the slightest bit curious to find out why I wish to speak to you?"

"As I have already told you the first time you called me, there is nothing you could possibly have to say that would interest me."

Steph took a half-step back so she could keep both David's and his mother's faces in her line of vision, taking his hand as she moved. His hand was clammy in hers, and it trembled noticeably. But his face was stone, and his voice was strong. She felt a powerful surge of pride in him, along with a cascade of understanding. *It's not just the letter, or the checks. This bullying witch has been* calling *him.*

Why couldn't he tell me?

"I'll make you a bargain," David's mother said, speaking only to David. "Give me five minutes, listen to what I have to tell you. Then you can decide if I should leave." She gave a brittle smile. "You might be surprised."

Steph looked at David, waiting for a signal. A breeze picked up, sending brisk March air into the house. David looked back at Steph, as if for guidance. All his strength from a moment ago might have blown away on the chilly breeze as well.

His mother, seizing on his hesitation, pushed harder. "Five minutes—inside, away from this awful wind. Surely that is not too much to ask?"

David still looked helpless, his resolve clearly crumbling under the weight of his mother's demand. His mother...his first abuser.

Who had been pestering him, despite being told not to.

Now she'd hunted him down in person, and refused to leave. Where would it stop?

"Five minutes," Steph decided. "Starting now."

David's mother looked at Steph with an air of clearly feigned respect. "At last, a voice of reason. Who knew." She shrugged, then added, "But where are my manners? I'm Kathryn Palmer." She put out a slender hand, unadorned except for a ring with the largest emerald Steph had ever seen, on the fourth finger.

Automatically, Steph reached out with her free hand and shook David's mother's hand. It was cold, and the sharp corners of the emerald scraped uncomfortably against her fingers. Kathryn gave a final assertive squeeze, just this side of painful, then let Steph's hand go.

"All right, come in," Steph said. She glanced up at David with an apology in her eyes; his expression was still that of a man lost. She hoped this had been the right decision. She hoped he would forgive her, if it wasn't.

Kathryn Palmer smiled her triumph and stepped into the hallway, glancing around, her keen gaze taking in their art, the slender table just inside the door, the high beamed ceilings, the imported Persian runner down the hall. "Well, you've done all right for yourself in spite of it all, I suppose," she said, taking a few more steps deeper into the house.

Steph pulled David to a halt. "I saw her letter, and the materials from your parents' company," she whispered. "We will talk about that after we get rid of her." She studied his face.

His eyes were wide, with surprise, fear, and—something else. Relief? Or was that just projection on her part? At least Steph's secret was finally out.

"Did you know she was coming here?" she added.

Kathryn had found her way to the big living room by now. "I'd kill for a cup of tea," she called back to them.

"She threatened to. I didn't think she'd really do it," David murmured.

Steph had so many questions, but right now, she also an emergency on her hands. The woman who was responsible for at least half of David's foundational trauma was making free with her house—*their* house—demanding hospitality, of all things.

After thirty years of no contact...until recently, anyway.

She shook her head and whispered to David, "We'll find out what she wants and then make her leave."

"I know what she wants," he said, mournfully. "Me."

"Hello?" Kathryn called, stepping back out into the hallway with a big saccharine smile on her face. "Oh, there you both are. Do come and sit with me, David, while Stephanie gets me a cup of tea."

Like hell I will, Steph thought, and grabbed David's hand again, leading him firmly down the hall toward his mother. "We'll both sit down with you for your five minutes, Kathryn—which have already started, by the way. Since you have come all this way from—wherever you have come from. And when those five minutes are up, you will leave. Without *tea*." She did not slow down, just marched David past his mother into the living room and led him to the couch. He sat, and she sat beside him, leaving Kathryn a choice of several plush side chairs, or a spindle-legged antique chair across from the sofa, beside the fireplace.

She chose the spindle chair. Steph could see her regathering her forces, could almost hear her thoughts as she dropped the tea demand and moved on. "Well. I must say, that's a warm welcome. Not that I'm surprised."

Steph just gazed back at her, still holding David's hand. This woman had so tortured David that he had broken off all contact with her, and his father, before she'd ever met him. Kathryn had of course never met Steph, had not come to their wedding, had not even sent congratulations. Kathryn had never known about their struggles to conceive, their attempt to adopt. Steph was frankly astonished, and a little alarmed, that she had been able to find their house.

Steph began to formulate an answer when David cleared his throat. "The clock is still ticking, Kathryn. You'd better say your piece, if you're going to."

"Well," his mother said again, rearing back a little in surprise. "I shall, then."

Steph squeezed her husband's hand; she knew what it must be costing him, just to be in the same room with this woman, much less to be speaking to her so firmly. Her pride in him warmed once more.

Kathryn took a breath and went on. "Your father has had another stroke. That makes three, plus a few little TIAs, the doctors think. He wants to see you—he *needs* to see you. This has gone on long enough; you will not be equipped to take over Palmer Investments without sufficient preparation. As you would know if you had looked at any of the materials we've sent you, six months ago, after the second stroke, he dissolved the board of directors, took the company private, and has made arrangements to leave the entire business to you and you alone. Without strings. Without encumbrances. But you need to step up immediately. You must return home *now*, so that you two can work on the transition while he's still capable of it."

Steph turned in time to see David shake his head. "If you think I have any intention of speaking to that man ever again in my life, much less in taking over Palmer Investments, you are mad."

Kathryn sniffed and waved a slender hand in dismissal. "I know you've had your differences…"

David turned to Steph. He masked it well, but she could see the call for help in his eyes. *I am on your side no matter what*, she thought, holding his sky-blue gaze. *I believe in you.*

Not even twenty-nine years of loving this man could bestow magical abilities to send her thoughts into his mind, but the love and trust on his face showed her that he understood anyway. Still, he trembled.

Steph squeezed his hand. "I'm right here," she said, as softly as she could. "And you've got this."

He stared at her another long moment, then seemed to steel himself. He let go of Steph's hand and got to his feet, squaring his shoulders as he stared down at his mother.

To the old biddy's credit (or shame), she stared right back at him, unflinching.

David swallowed audibly, and then began to speak to Kathryn. His voice was soft at first, but gained strength as he went on. "Let me make this clear, as I did thirty years ago, and again much more recently. Dave Senior does not need, or want, to see me. *You* do not want to see me. You two have wanted nothing to do with me since I told you in no uncertain terms that running an investment company, *your* investment company, was not something I was ever going to do."

"But your intelligence—your head for numbers—" she started.

David shook his head vigorously. "Don't even. You've both thought I was a freak from my earliest childhood. I know you were disappointed not to have any other, better, more *normal* children. But you were stuck with me, only me. Too bad. Once you stifled your disappointment and decided to make the best of a bad situation, you pushed me into math and finance, so I could take over the family business someday. Not that you ever asked me if I wanted that, of course. Weirdly, I found that I loved the math and finance—just not the business. Never the business.

"I still don't love the business—*any* business. Do you know what I love? You don't," he continued without pausing, "because you don't know me. You don't want to know me. You've never wanted to know me."

"Of course I do," she said, her voice trembling artfully. "You're my *son*."

"Could have fooled me." He shook his head, still standing over her. "I love the numbers—their purity, their patterns, the magic they make. The play of them, the beauty. Dave, and you, love the *money*."

Kathryn glanced meaningfully around the elegant, comfortable room, but again David spoke before she could comment.

"Yes, I've done well for myself. Even being a behind-the-scenes analyst pays pretty well, if you're good at it, and I've made even more money playing the markets independently. I'm proud of how well I've done, and the comfortable life I've made—not just for me, but far more importantly, for my wife, Steph. The only person on this planet who has ever believed in me wholeheartedly—who loves me for exactly who I am, not who she wishes I were, or thinks she can turn me into someday if she pushes hard enough."

Steph felt tears pricking at the corners of her eyes. *Oh, David*, she thought.

Kathryn was just glaring up at him, her sculpted chin quivering slightly.

"You can go back to Dave and tell him all this," David went on. "Tell him you're both thirty—forty—fifty years too late to make this any different. Tell him you made your beds when I was just a child, and now you get to lie in them. Tell him that *Jonathan* can take over Palmer Investments, and with my blessing. Dave always loved him better than his own son anyway."

Kathryn's chin now fairly trembled. "Jonathan quit five months ago."

David paused, looking shocked. "*Jonathan?* Quit? Dave's own little mini-me, his sycophant-in-training, the golden boy I never was—he quit?" Then, bizarrely, David laughed. Steph hadn't seen such fierce joy on his face since…well, since the last time they'd made love, to be honest. "Why in the world did his little minion leave, after all these years? Wait—you said Dave took the company private, and cut him out of the line of succession. That must have stung."

Kathryn narrowed her eyes. "Would you sit down, please. I'm growing weary of craning up at you."

David snorted, but then took a seat beside Steph again. He reached for her hand; she took his, and found it steady and strong.

"I am sure I don't know Jonathan's reasons for leaving Palmer Investments," Kathryn said, "and it does not matter. He was not family, not blood; he was never suitable for running the family business. You are. If you would get over your little snit, you would realize that it would be best for all concerned if you were to resume your proper place."

"Thirty years of no-contact estrangement is not a *little snit*. And my entire family is sitting right here beside me." He squeezed Steph's hand; she squeezed back. "Furthermore, your five minutes are more than up. We're hosting a dinner party tonight; the guests will be arriving soon. It's time for you to walk back out that door and onto the next ferry, and out of our lives forever."

"Ferry." Kathryn snorted. "As if."

David rolled his eyes. "Oh, of course, I forgot: the great Kathryn Palmer is far too important and rarefied to subject herself to a public ferry. What, did you bring the corporate jet?"

She reared back just a half-inch; her nostrils narrowed as if a bad odor had filled the room. "The miserable excuse for an airport on this island maintains that its runway is *too short* for the corporate jet. I had to come via some sort of shabby little commuter airline—Kensington or something." She shook her head in disgust.

David got to his feet again; this time, Steph rose with him. "Well then," David said, "you can then find your way back to the airport and take *Kenmore Air* right back off again. Because this conversation is over." He took a step closer, looming above his mother.

She got up as well, pulling the shreds of her dignity about her narrow shoulders and lifting her chin. "Fine. I will leave you to think about what we have discussed here. It's clear that emotions are running rather high at the moment, but I think given time, you will find—"

"No," David said, quite calmly. "There is nothing further to discuss, and there will be no more thinking about things. Steph and I are going back to preparing for our dinner party, and you are leaving our home and island forever. You will stop mailing me materials and checks from the business, and stop phoning and texting me as well; I will take out a restraining order if I need to. And tell Dave…" He paused, then said, "Tell Dave not to bother us either."

Kathryn's eyes widened as David pointed to the doorway leading to the hall. "You don't even want to send any wishes for his speedy healing?"

David merely kept pointing.

Kathryn huffed, clutching her Hermès bag to her side, and walked down the hall toward the front door.

Steph and David followed her, side by side. At the door, Kathryn turned, seemed about to say something more, but, wisely, thought better of it.

After David closed the door behind her, he turned and leaned against it. Steph looked up at him, ready for anything—a breakdown, a fit of hysteria, her husband collapsing into a puddle on the floor.

But he just looked back at her, calmly. He was almost smiling.

And then he was fully smiling. His brow unfurrowed; he dropped ten years, just like that. "Oh my god," he said. "I can't believe I did that."

"You were amazing," Steph said softly.

He opened his arms and pulled her into them, holding her tightly. "*You* were amazing-er," he said, and then…then he laughed.

She wasn't even sure it was laughter at first—he was trembling so hard, it was shaking them both. She had to draw back and look at his face, but yes, he was laughing—with relief, with release. It was unlike his laughter of a minute earlier: less fierce, but more joyous.

And it was nearly tears, as well.

"Oh my god," he said again. "I feel…I can't even describe it. It was like pulling a splinter out of my heart—it hurt, so much, but the relief…"

Steph felt relief flood through her as well. "You were magnificent. My David."

"I didn't know I could speak to her like that. I didn't know I had any of that in me."

Steph never lied to David, so she didn't want to say *Oh, I knew you did*; but as she searched for what to say instead, she suddenly realized that it was true. He wasn't weak, or cowardly; he had been very badly hurt, from his childhood onward; and he certainly got frightened, especially when assholes were bullying him; but she had never doubted the strength in him.

What was new now was his finding his voice. And, oh, at such a moment.

"I have never doubted you," she told him.

His eyes shone with emotion as he pulled her into another strong hug. They stood together in the front hall for a long moment, just holding onto each other, rocking gently.

After he released her, he looked down into her face and said, "She pulled you out of the kitchen; do you need to get back to it? Can I do anything to help you?"

"She did get me at kind of a bad moment," Steph said. "But David, this was huge. We can cancel soup group tonight—everyone would understand if we told them something came up."

"No, you're so far along, and you've done so much prep for this one—"

She shook her head. "Seriously, don't even think about that. How are *you* right now? I don't want to rush off and ignore you, and then fill your house with company tonight of all nights."

He kept gazing down at her, clearly thinking. Finally, he said,

"You know? I think I'm…I don't want to say 'fine,' but I think I'm okay. And I also think a house full of people tonight sounds… kind of weirdly comforting."

Who are you and what have you done with my husband? she thought. "If you change your mind, I can still cancel right up until like a half-hour before."

He shook his head. "No. If I need to get away from people after they get here, I'll do that. But for now, let me know how I can help."

She studied him for another long moment. He really did look okay. Maybe it was the shock of it, and he'd fall apart later. As he said, though, he could go hide in his study if he needed to. "Well, that did actually take time I didn't have to spare. I could use a hand, if you're willing."

"Of course. Anything."

She smiled. "Wait till you hear what it is before you agree."

"There's nothing you can ask me to do that'll be harder than what I just did."

"Well, that's a fair point," she conceded.

"So what is it?"

She started leading him back down the hall. "Remember how to make pie crust?"

"Yeah, I do. You need a pie crust made?"

"Just rolled out and put in the pie pans, and then keep an eye on them as they bake. There are several of them."

"I might need a refresher…"

"Don't worry," Steph said, as they stepped into the kitchen. "I'll be right here with you. But if I don't get started on the fillings—not to mention finishing the soup—I'm never going to make it in time."

"I've got it," he said, heading for the pastry station.

She got him set up there, and then kept checking on him, making sure he was really okay and had everything he needed, until he gently, sweetly, but firmly assured her that he was just fine, and moreover, he knew what he was doing. "It's not going to be any help to you if you're just hovering over me," he said. "Do your fillings."

"Okay, yes. Thank you." She made herself get busy on the other side of the kitchen, only glancing over at him every now and then. He was clearly doing fine, not even managing to spackle the entire area with flour as she always seemed to do. He had, indeed, done a lot of baking a decade or more ago, before they'd moved here full-time.

Back when they had done a lot more things together.

Was it possible to find that place again? To not turn back the clock, exactly, but reset where it was heading in the future? Steph had despaired of it, these last few weeks.

But now? She started to feel a resurgence of hope.

Across the room, David began to hum softly as he worked.

Chapter 10

STEPH

When Julie and Gavin rang the doorbell, David not only didn't sneak off to hide in his study, he actually went and let them in, shepherding them into the kitchen and getting them glasses of wine. Steph was amused to see Gavin's nonplussed expression; she could almost read his thoughts: *What's going on here?*

Julie, at least, had encountered David's social side—however rare and fleeting—before. She sat comfortably by him at the kitchen island, asking him questions about his work, acting like everything was normal and fine.

Which it was. Right? It was normal and fine to face down your estranged mother, then bake for what remained of the afternoon before hosting a dinner party?

Steph shook her head and returned to her soup, which smelled heavenly. Or maybe that was the savory pies, baking in the oven. The trick with the scallop one had been the timing: scallops do not like to be overcooked; in fact they hardly like to be cooked at all. Steph had settled on fully baking the bottom crust *and* partially baking rounds of top crust on their own cookie sheet, then cooking the filling's sauce and other ingredients before returning the assembled pies to the oven for barely long enough to warm the raw scallops through. It required most of her attention; she was watching through the glass of the oven door for any sign of excess bubbling, so when the doorbell rang again, David once more got up to answer it.

Within ten minutes, all the pies were cooling on the rack, and the whole soup group was crammed in the kitchen, laughing and talking and drinking together.

With David.

And it felt perfectly natural, just as it did a bit later when they all gathered around the dining room table for the meal. Conversation flowed easily. Even Ron didn't snipe at Alicia, though that could have been because she sat at the opposite corner of the table from him. Whatever the reason, it was a nice change.

Matt, sitting beside Steph, told her, "If anyone had ever, before tonight, asked me if I would want to eat pie with scallops in it, I would have said no way."

"Or tofu pot pie!" Alicia said.

Steph laughed. "Even if they had been sure to mention that they were savory pies?"

"Even then. But god, this is amazing." Matt underscored his words by taking another hearty bite.

"I feel a little sorry for my soup," Steph said, already second-guessing her decision to make the simpler recipe, though there would have been not a tiny chance she could have gotten the more complicated one done in time, even with David's help. "I hope it's not jealous that everyone's wolfing down the pies."

"Well, it is Pi Day," Lynne put in, from the other side of the table. "But don't worry—I'm already on my second bowl of soup."

"Oh good," Steph said.

Lynne gave her a wink. "I see you didn't actually make a decision on the pies after all. So much for needing my taste-testing help."

"Choosing to make all four is a decision!" Steph protested.

"Wait, Lynne got to taste all these before?" Julie asked, looking bereft.

"I did invite you," Steph said. "But you had to work."

"If you had explained that it was a *pie-tasting* lunch…"

"It's a next-door-neighbor perk," Lynne told Julie with a smile. "As is the freedom to give my neighbor career advice," she said, turning to Steph with an encouraging smile. "Have you done any more thinking about your big dinners?"

Now the whole table was listening, interested. *Crap*, Steph thought, *what do I do now?* She still felt that hosting them here at the house would be amazing, but David had clearly hated the idea. And here he was just down the table, looking back at her…

She met his eyes, but saw none of the fear or stress from when they'd talked about this before. He gave her a small nod and said, "Go ahead and tell them about your good idea."

"Really?" she asked him.

"Yeah." He smiled shyly. "We can talk more about it, but… yeah."

Wow. "Okay," Steph said, and told the group her thinking. "I wouldn't commit to anything large, at first," she concluded, "not until we saw how it went—not just how popular the dinners might be, but how it feels doing them here, and what the neighbors think." She glanced at Lynne. "The *other* neighbors, that is; I know what this one thinks."

"You certainly do," Lynne agreed. "And I am so happy to hear how far you've gotten with this!"

"Oh, not far at all," Steph protested. "I haven't done any real research."

"You've done the important part," Lynne said softly, and did she shoot a quick glance at David as she did? "Just admitting to yourself that you want to do this: that's the biggest step. Everything after that is details."

Throughout the whole conversation, Ron was watching her raptly from his side of the table. Nothing unusual in that: everyone was watching her as she told them her plans. What was weird, though, was the avidity of his gaze—and she wasn't picking up any Pepe le Pew vibes, either. He was almost smiling, as though…as though he were proud?

Well, he was a retired professor, having spent a career shepherding young people, helping them grow. Maybe that expanded to include pride in his friends when they did big important things? But she hadn't forgotten that weird episode at his house last fall, not to mention the frequent, obvious tension between him and Alicia.

Alicia, for her part, was smiling happily at Steph. "I think this is so exciting," she said, as Steph caught her gaze. "If you need any help with this, definitely let me know. I can draw up your menus or something."

"You're already too busy writing up the recipes for our cookbook!" Julie protested, with a laugh.

"I'm getting faster!" Alicia said. "And if the dinners don't start till the summer, I'll certainly be done with the cookbook in time to help." She turned back to Steph. "Just think about it and let me know. I can do other things too."

"Thank you," Steph said, and then, to the table at large, "Actually, thank you everyone—for believing in me, for encouraging me. I know this doesn't seem like a big thing—"

Protests all around now, as everyone laughingly disagreed with her.

"Okay, okay, fine," Steph said, waving down their acclaim. "It's a huge thing, and you're all awesome friends, the very best; and who wants coffee or tea?" She got up as she spoke and headed for the kitchen.

Now it's me running away from crowds, she thought ruefully, as she filled the coffee maker with water. Out in the dining room, she could hear laughter and the clanking of dishes, and then a minute later, footsteps behind her.

"Thanks—" she started, turning around expecting to see David with an armload of plates and bowls, but it was Ron. "Oh hey."

At least he had carried in his own dishes. He deposited them in the sink and walked closer to Steph, still with that odd, proud smile on his face. "I just wanted to say that I think your idea is superlative," he said.

"Thank you," she said, stepping away to get the coffee beans from the fridge. "I'm excited about it."

"Of course you will reserve places at the table for your soup group!"

She nodded, and returned to the coffee station, getting the bean grinder out of its cubby. "Of course I will."

Ron took another step closer to her—still not quite invading her personal space, but one more step would do it. Was she going to have to deal with this after all? Today, of all days? *Really, Ron?* "These evenings at your house," he said, "the dinners you cook for us all—I just want to say, they are a highlight of my life."

"Um." Steph filled the grinder with beans and closed the lid. "Thanks." Then she held up the grinder with what she hoped was an apologetic expression and pushed the button, filling the kitchen with its awful noise.

Ron merely waited, smiling.

She could only grind for so long without taking the beans past "grounds" to "espresso" and then "dust." She stopped, tipping the grounds into the filter, and pushed the button to start the machine brewing. Now what?

Right, tea. She stepped over to the stove and picked up the kettle. But filling it at the sink would mean walking right past Ron—either brushing past him uncomfortably closely, or awkwardly circumnavigating the island. So she froze, indecisive, and suddenly angry. What did he *want* from her? What was he even thinking he was doing in here? Were they supposed to, what, sneak a kiss or something with their spouses and best friends in the next room?

"Your friendship means so much to me," he said.

"I like you and Alicia too," she said, taking a step back. Maybe she should go around the island after all. As his face fell only very slightly, she couldn't help remembering their past mild flirtation, how much she'd enjoyed his company, his quick wit and intellectual prowess. His obvious regard for her. *Six months ago I might actually have considered it*, she thought wryly.

Ron found his conversational footing again. "So I was wondering if we might—"

Just then, thank god, another set of footsteps sounded in the doorway.

Steph turned gratefully to see Alicia, holding a stack of plates and looking at Ron with an unreadable expression.

"Oh thanks!" Steph said to her, probably way too volubly but also *what the hell?* "You can just set those in the sink. And help me with the coffee cups?"

Alicia's gaze lingered on Ron for a moment longer before she said, "Right, happy to. Ron, you want to gather cups with me?"

"Of *course* I do," he said, casting a final, fond glance at Steph before helping his wife.

Steph took a deep breath after they left the room. She was going to have to do something about this, wasn't she?

Well, crisis averted, for the moment, anyway. She filled the kettle and put it on the stove, then began gathering cream, sugar, teabags and spoons to take out to the table.

JULIE

JULIE HAD FINALLY made the frosted lemon pound cake she'd promised last fall. She sliced it up right at the table and served it around on Steph's pretty flowered dessert plates as Steph brought out the coffee and tea. Alicia and—for some reason—Ron helped distribute the cups. Maybe Ron was trying to get his act together? That would be nice. The last soup group, when he'd made Alicia cry on their drive over, had been awkward for everyone.

"Oh man," Matt said, taking a big bite of cake. "This is *amazing*."

"It's the perfect follow-on to the citrusy, lemongrassy meal," Lynne added, around a generous mouthful of her own.

Julie had to agree. And the recipe hadn't even been as complicated as she remembered. "I'll make this again anytime you-all like," she promised, to general acclaim around the table.

"May I have a second piece?" David asked, nudging his empty plate toward her.

"Of course!" Julie cut him a thick slice as others passed her their plates.

After only a few more minutes, forks scraped again on cleaned plates, and Gavin discreetly put a hand on Julie's thigh under the table, giving her a gentle but pointed squeeze. "What say we sneak out of here soon?" he whispered in her ear, sending a rush of delightful warmth through her.

"Mmm, sounds good," she whispered back.

Steph couldn't have overheard them; perhaps she just read their body language. She got up and started gathering the dessert plates. David followed suit, clearing the coffee cups, and the whole party got up and began making their exits.

On the way to her car, Gavin pulled her close for a kiss which quickly grew passionate. Julie didn't want to stop him...but she also didn't want to do this *here*. "Let's get back to town," she said, pulling back and smiling at him.

"Right. Town. Your house. Your bed," he said, his voice husky.

She chuckled softly and unlocked her car. "I couldn't agree more. But try to hold it together till we get there—I don't want to drive off the road."

"I'll do my best."

As she pulled out, he added, "Despite my sudden, ah, urgent need, I have to say that I did really enjoy the evening."

Julie laughed out loud. "I'm glad. Life can't be all bed sports; we need meals and friends too."

"David seems like a nice guy. I haven't really gotten to know him before."

"None of us have, all that well. He doesn't usually stay for the whole evening, if he shows up at all."

"He seemed to be enjoying himself," Gavin said.

Julie nodded. "He and Steph have been working on some issues in their marriage. She told Alicia and me a little bit about it a while back. Maybe one of the things they're trying is doing more stuff together as a couple."

"That's nice. They both seemed—well, in a good place, somehow."

Julie thought about it as she drove. "I know what you mean. He usually seems more nervous and shy, and she usually seems more…I don't know, like an island unto herself. A friendly, social island, but still. Independent. Self-sufficient."

"Exactly," Gavin said. "I noticed how he encouraged her to tell us all about her plan for hosting community dinners. She seemed surprised and really pleased."

"She was adorable! Actually, they both were. I loved how they looked at each other. I hadn't seen that before."

"It's nice when things work out."

"I wonder if Alicia and Ron are going to be next," Julie said. "They also seemed more at ease tonight. Or at least Ron seemed mellower."

"I have to say, Ron is an acquired taste," Gavin observed dryly.

"It helps if you're a wine enthusiast," Julie said, laughing. "His grumpy old professor act is easier to take if you're sipping one of his fabulous vintages."

Gavin shook his head, smiling. "Too bad for me, then, I guess."

MATT

MATT HAD TRIED all evening to figure out how to keep his promise to Megan, to talk to Julie about the whole McLeod issue and suss out her emotional state around it. The trouble was, he had waited for the issue to come up organically, but it hadn't. And Julie seemed so relaxed and happy that he hadn't wanted to ruin that by bringing it up himself.

He'd thought about telling her the truth—that he'd been talking to Megan and she'd been worried about her mom—but...then he'd have had to tell her that he'd been talking to Megan.

But that was fine! Right? He could talk to Megan, there was nothing wrong with that. Julie knew they'd gone out a few times over the new year, and she hadn't seemed weird about it.

So why did *he* feel weird about it? He and Megan weren't dating; they'd discussed it and agreed not to. But they theoretically could date...if things were different...

Right?

There had never been any spark between Julie and Matt; they were just friends, always had been, long before she'd gotten together with Gavin. So it wouldn't be like he was throwing over the mother for the daughter.

He could just tell Megan that her mom seemed happy, and that the issue hadn't come up. But he'd kind of promised to do more than that...

What was the matter with him? Why couldn't he just talk to his friend?

But before he knew it, everyone had scraped their dessert plates clean, then gathered in the front hall to put on their coats, thank Steph, and declare the evening a resounding success. Julie and Gavin were the first ones out the door and into their car, so that was that.

Matt turned to David, standing beside him. "It was good to spend some time with you, dude," he said, shaking his hand.

"Likewise," David said, ducking his head a bit in shyness but also smiling.

Huh, that was strange, that David had hung with them the whole evening, Matt realized. He'd been so caught up in his own dilemma that he hadn't really processed that fact. Well, Steph had seemed happier lately as well; maybe they were working some stuff through. He hoped so.

It was encouraging when couples worked stuff through, rather than just, oh, say, running away.

Matt waited for the familiar wave of anger and grief about Heather to flood through him, but he felt only the faintest echo of last fall's pain. *Huh*, he thought again.

Steph pulled him in for a goodbye hug. "Thanks so much for the fruit salad. It was perfect."

"My pleasure," he said, and kept his mouth shut about the fact that it had been a platter from Costco, arranged into one of his own salad bowls. What Steph didn't know would never hurt her.

STEPH

STEPH STOOD NEXT to David in the front hall after the last of the group had left. "That was such a nice evening," she said, putting her arm around his waist. "Thank you for staying."

He squeezed her close. "You're welcome; it was great. Your pies—and your soup—were delicious."

"*Our* pies," she said, smiling up at him.

"Our pies." They heard the last car start, and drive off. "I'll help you clean up."

Steph quashed her immediate instinct to say *No thanks, I've got it.* "Sure, let's do it."

An extra pair of hands did make a difference. Within twenty minutes, the dishwasher was humming quietly, the extra food was all put away, the pastry station was wiped clean, and the soup pot and various frying pans were drying on the stove. "Want to sit in the living room for a minute?" Steph asked, not quite ready to go to bed yet. Not quite ready to close the books on this most singular of days.

Not even sure what was supposed to happen next. Except that

boy howdy, they really did need to talk.

"Yes. I would like that very much."

Soon they were seated in their usual places before the fire, short glasses of brandy before them. "I'm sorry I snooped in your office," she started, in the interest of tearing off the band-aid, "and I'm also sorry I didn't ask you about what I found right away."

David nodded, staring at the fire. After a pause that stretched so long she began to wonder if that would be his only response, he said, "I'm sorry I didn't tell you that she'd started sending me stuff. I just...I wanted to, but I couldn't figure out how. But mostly I wanted it to just not be happening."

"I get it," she said.

He turned to her with a rueful smile. "I wanted to not have to have any of the conversations that we're now obviously going to have—about my childhood, about all the things they did to me."

"We don't have to do any of it tonight," she said. "And I don't need a whole bunch more details about your past—I don't need you to dredge up old wounds. What I *do* need is to know what's going on now, and in the future."

"I was terrified that she would show up here. I couldn't even think about it half the time, I was so scared. But it's weird," he said, musingly. "After she did it—the worst possible thing, the thing I'd been dreading for months—I feel...a lot less scared. Maybe even less wounded."

"I think our imagination can make things so much more frightening than any reality. In your mind, it was all the pain, all the trauma, the whole lifetime of stuff she—they—did to you. In reality, it was one manipulative old woman with an expensive purse trying to tell a grown man what to do, and that grown man telling her no."

He chuckled. "I'm probably still on some sort of high from telling her off like that, but I sort of feel like I *can* talk about things. With you, at least."

"I am always happy to listen to anything you want to tell me.

Anything."

He reached over and took her hand. "Thank you. But you're right: not tonight."

"It's been a long day." They sat quietly for a minute, holding hands and watching the fire. "And you know it is always safe to tell me stuff, right?" she added. "Even if it's hard stuff."

"I do know that." He turned to look at her, his eyes earnest. "I…" He shrugged. "I will do better. I'm sorry."

"Don't beat yourself up," she said gently. "I just wanted to make sure that was clear."

"It is. And thank you."

"You're welcome. I love you."

"I love you too." He looked down at their joined hands and then back up at her. "I still can't quite believe she hunted me down all the way up here on Orcas Island. Like I said, part of me just didn't believe it was real. That there was even anything to tell you. Or at least, that's what I kept telling myself."

Steph nodded. "That does make sense."

They sat in silence for a while longer this time. Steph savored the peace, the calm after the storm—both storms, the thunder and lightning of Kathryn's visit and the happy whirlwind of the dinner party. Eventually, she said, "You really do seem okay, which is kind of amazing to me."

"Honestly? I think I am, but I also don't entirely know." He let go of her hand and leaned forward to pick up his snifter, taking a small sip. "Or, I guess a better way of putting it would be our old standby: Yes, No, I don't know." He gave a rueful grin.

"That also makes sense." She sipped her own drink, then sat back and leaned into him again. "It really was nice," she added after a minute, "to have you there at soup group tonight."

"Well, after working so hard on those pie crusts, I couldn't just let you all eat them without me." He grinned. Then he sobered and added, "I do like all those people—well, most of them—but to tell you the truth, it was also very distracting. And I needed the distraction."

"Ah."

He nodded. "There were a few times when I was tempted to go retreat, but then I would just ruminate about Kathryn's visit. Even if I was working, I can do that with only a small part of my brain. Being social...takes a lot more of my brain, more of my attention. It's harder work, but that was just what I needed tonight."

Steph's heart broke, just a tiny bit, at hearing so clearly stated what she already knew perfectly well: that hanging out with friends, even people he liked a lot, was hard work for David. She understood it, to a degree—she would have to, after spending more than half her life with the man—but a part of her would never truly get it, all the way down. For her, the work of preparing food and cleaning up after it was a bit tiring, sure, even though she also loved the creative act and the delight everyone took in her efforts; but she found socializing itself to be stimulating, energizing.

Why did introverts marry extroverts? You saw it everywhere. Yes, opposites attract, but my goodness.

"Did you have any fun, though?" she asked, trying not to sound plaintive.

Trying and failing, apparently. David took her hand again and looked earnestly into her eyes. "I did," he said. "Really. I like Julie's boyfriend Gavin a lot—maybe it's because he works in a library, but his energy is calm. He's easy to be around."

"Good, I'm glad." She smiled at him.

"And I had some nice conversations with Matt, and I think Alicia is a really interesting person. She's...less calm, though."

"She is a little high-strung, I agree." *And with good reason*, Steph added silently.

"I mean, everyone was nice—it's a great group, and I've known most of them for years, at a certain level. I do like them, and I'm comfortable having them here. As comfortable as I can be with anyone who's not you."

"Aww."

"It's not that I don't like people—any people, really," he went on. "It's that they wear me out." He shrugged. "I'm so exhausted right now, but it's nice, sitting here with you."

"I agree, I like this too. But I'm tired as well; we can go to bed anytime."

"Soon."

They sat sipping their brandies for another few minutes. Steph felt herself continuing to relax, degree by degree. Eventually, she finished her drink and set the empty glass on the coffee table. Turning to David, she was about to suggest they turn in when the doorbell rang.

They stared at each other. "That's not…" she started.

"She better not have come back here," David said, his voice a low growl. "If she dares, I *will* call the sheriff's department."

"We won't let her in. I don't care if she has to sleep in the woods, she's not setting foot in this house ever again." She got up. "You stay here; I'll look through the peephole. It's probably just Lynne." But Lynne went to bed early…and she would have texted, not walked over.

Unless it was some kind of emergency?

Steph's heart beat more rapidly as she approached the front door. The porch light was still on; whoever it was would know they were being peered at, most likely.

She put her eye to the peephole—and then took a breath and quickly opened the door.

Alicia stood on the porch, her eyes red from crying, a spot of dark makeup under one eye (at least, Steph hoped it was makeup). She carried a duffel bag in one hand; a laptop case was slung over her shoulder. "I'm so sorry—" she started, but Steph interrupted her.

"Come in and don't apologize for anything."

She swept Alicia along toward the living room. David met

them halfway down the hallway, joining them on Alicia's other side. Together, they escorted her to the couch, taking seats on either side of her.

"Did he hit you?" Steph asked.

"No! God, no." She sniffled, wiping away a tear with her forearm. "But we fought—we've been fighting more and more lately, and I just—I've had it. He's not going to change, and I can't do it anymore. I just suddenly knew I couldn't sleep even one more night under the same roof as him. So, um…can I stay here for a night or two, just to figure things out?"

"Yes, of course, as long as you need," Steph said, as David nodded and added, "Yes, absolutely."

"Thank you." Alicia took a deep breath. "Oh god." She blinked and looked at Steph. "I didn't get you guys out of bed, did I?"

"No, we were still up. Can I get you anything at all? We were just finishing up some brandies."

"I…brandy sounds good but I don't know if it would be smart…"

"I'll get you a brandy and a glass of water, and you can choose." Steph started to get up, but David was already rising.

"I'll get them," he said. "You stay here with Alicia."

"Thank you guys, both," Alicia said, as David left the room. "I'm really sorry, but I didn't know where else to go, and I know you have several guest rooms…"

"It's really, really okay, and I meant it about not apologizing," Steph said. "If I'm not the kind of person that a good friend feels she can flee to at any time, day or night, then I'm doing something wrong."

Alicia pulled her into a sudden fierce hug. "You *are* that kind of person. I didn't even consider going anywhere else." When she let go, she said, "Even though…you know Ron has a crush on you, right?"

Steph smiled uncomfortably. "It's been painfully obvious, yes."

"I'm sorry about that too," Alicia said with a grimace. "And I know—don't apologize, and I especially know that I'm not re-sponsible for other people's behavior, but—I married the man, you know?"

"I do know." Steph took Alicia's hand. "You married him a long time ago. Everybody changes—for better and for worse." She cringed. "Ugh, sorry, no wedding-vows pun intended. What I mean is we change in every way—we're not static, nobody is. Sometimes, marriages grow stronger when the people in them change; sometimes they fall apart. Sometimes people weather the changes and just grow the marriage differently. It looks to me like you both changed over the years, and what was once function-al...isn't anymore."

"It hasn't been for a long time," Alicia said. "I thought I could just...live my own life, like you do. Or like you seemed to...I know things are different lately."

Steph glanced at the doorway to the hall. David should have been back with Alicia's drinks by now; was he giving them an extra moment? "I was living my own life, and it wasn't work-ing either. We...it's been a bit of a bumpy road, and it's still go-ing on—and it's not all mine to tell—but we're still working on changing the direction of a lot of things. I have hope, now, where I didn't for a long time."

"I'm so happy for you," Alicia said. "David and you seem so much more at peace with each other. More intimate. The whole feeling is different."

Steph smiled. "You're right, it is."

"I think that's part of why I was pushing back," Alicia said. "It kind of touched a nerve in me, seeing you happier lately, the stuff you told me and Julie at the pizza place a while back—it got me thinking. And then seeing both of you tonight—well, like I said, I'd had it." She gave a watery smile. "Ron didn't want to hear any of it, of course."

"Ron is..." Steph paused.

"You can say it, whatever it is," Alicia said with a sad laugh.

"Though there's no need to: I've thought everything there is to think about him, and more." She sighed. "And when I came into the kitchen and saw him cornering you tonight, I guess that was the last straw."

Steph just nodded. She couldn't exactly deny it, could she? He had indeed cornered her. And he had been on the verge of proposing...something.

"I brought it up on the drive home," Alicia went on. "He of course denied it—he'd just been in there helping with the coffee, what was I accusing him of, was I crazy? Insane with jealousy? I told him it wasn't just tonight, that he was clearly fixated on you and that it was making everyone uncomfortable, and would he please stop it. Well, the more he denied it, the more I wanted to somehow prove I was right—oh, you don't want to hear the whole blow-by-blow. Metaphorically speaking!" she added, with a laugh.

"It's all right, tell me anything you want to," Steph said. "Sometimes getting it all out helps."

"Ugh, not this, it's just dumb. Anyway we were still fighting when we got home, and he was still doing that thing where he implies that I'm stupid and crazy and hysterical and whatever-all-else, and he's the calm and rational and intelligent one—never mind that he's shouting by now, because obviously Crazy Alicia provoked him into it—and I just...something fell over inside of me. It almost felt like that, like a physical thing. A switch got turned, or a line of energy shut off, leaving only darkness. And I just thought, *I'm done. I can't be married to this man anymore; I can't live in this house anymore.* So I walked right past him into the bedroom, grabbed some stuff, and left."

"I'm glad you did."

David finally returned with the drinks, on a tray with the brandy bottle. "Sorry to take so long," he said, setting the tray on the coffee table in front of Alicia.

"Oh, thank you," Alicia said, picking up the water glass and draining it down. "God, I didn't realize how thirsty I was."

"Shall I refill it?" David was still standing.

"No, that's good." She picked up the brandy snifter and took a small sip. "Mmm, that's good too."

"Steph?" David lifted the brandy bottle and nodded at her empty glass.

"Just a drop."

He gave her and himself a few drops, then sat in one of the easy chairs.

"Thank you," Steph said to him, hoping her eyes carried the larger meaning as well, the *Thank you for giving us the extra time.*

"My pleasure," he said, and raised his glass in their direction.

Steph was glad to see that Alicia sipped her brandy, and that she was clearly calming down, more by the minute.

"I'm exhausted," Alicia said, when her drink was nearly gone. "You guys must be tired too. I don't mean to keep you up after the day you've had."

And you don't know the half of it, Steph thought. "The guest rooms are already made up—do you want the one you used before, or a different one? I should warn you, our other guest room only has twin beds, and you have to use the bathroom in the hall."

Alicia looked at her. "You know? I hadn't thought about it, but I'd be happier in the other room. A twin bed sounds fantastic right now, and I don't care about the bathroom."

"Of course." Alicia had only spent one night with Ron in that room, but if she were looking for an absolutely clean break, this made sense.

Steph got up. "Well, let's get you settled. Sounds like we could all use some sleep."

Both David and Alicia rose as well. "Thank you again," Alicia said.

"You are very, very welcome," Steph told her.

IN BED, STEPH snuggled up to David's back, putting an arm around his waist. He put his hand over hers and held her to him.

"What a day," she murmured.

"Indeed." He stroked her arm gently. "I'm glad she felt comfortable coming here," he added, after a minute.

"Oh, me too. Poor Alicia."

"I told you Ron was…not quite right."

Steph sighed. "I know there's a guy we all like in there somewhere; I remember getting to know him over the years. He's always been a little edgy, but in the last year or so…he's gotten worse."

"He's obviously going through something." David made a quiet *hmph* sound, not quite laughter but close to it. "People do, you know. And they don't even always tell their wives."

"I have *no idea* what you're talking about," she murmured, deadpan.

"Mmm, of course you don't." He sighed as well, and turned onto his back, holding onto her arm as he moved so that she would know he wasn't trying to push her away. Then he chuckled softly.

"What is it?" she asked.

"Oh, it's nothing—I'm just wondering if all our dinner parties are now going to feature sleepovers. I'm not sure I'll want your community dinners all camped out here!"

Steph laughed. "I think a twenty-person slumber party would be a bit much even for me."

"That's good," he said sleepily. "Anyway…goodnight." He turned and gave her a soft kiss.

She returned the kiss gratefully. "Thank you for everything today."

"You're welcome and thank you. I love you." He smiled at her, and closed his eyes.

"I love you too."

Was he okay? He looked so at peace, from what she could see

in the faint moonlight. He had pulled a splinter out of his heart, he said. How long would that take to heal? Would things really, truly start to change now?

She didn't want to ask him yet again how he was feeling, whether he wanted to talk. He knew she was here to listen to whatever he wanted to say, whenever he found the need to say it. She didn't need to remind him.

For now, they could just sleep, and deal with everything in the fullness of time.

Right?

David answered her thoughts by snoring softly.

Steph smiled at him in the darkness and curled up against his side, letting her own thoughts drift off into slumber.

RON

RON SAT ALONE in the big house, before the cold fireplace.

After Alicia had stormed off in her huff, he had waited for her to come back, with her tail between her legs.

He would forgive her, of course; they were married, after all, and it wasn't like he'd done anything wrong. Steph and he were just friends—there was no *there* there.

Sure, he admired her, but who wouldn't? Everyone loved Steph.

When had Alicia become so insecure? Surely she hadn't been that way when he'd met her. He'd greatly admired her spunk and independence. He'd actually had to woo her, to convince her to even give him a try.

When she didn't come back after thirty minutes, Ron had sighed, and begun getting ready for bed. He dragged it out, but she still didn't come back.

Where could she have gone? Nothing was open this time of night—not on a Sunday in March, not on Orcas Island. Was she going to sleep in her car?

He hoped she hadn't wasted a pile of money checking into

a hotel or something. That would be just like her: impetuous, spendthrift. Yes, they could afford it, but they had a budget for a reason: to agree on common expenditures.

He would talk to her about this, after she apologized.

Teeth brushed, wearing his pajamas, Ron had walked through the living room, turning out the last of the lights, when somehow, without even consciously deciding to, he had sunk down into this chair before the cold fireplace. In the dark.

He'd thought he'd heard something—her car? A footstep on the porch?

Of course it had been nothing.

But here he sat. Alone. In the dark.

I should go to bed, he thought, but he still did not move. Like Vladimir and Estragon. Waiting. It infuriated him, but he was stuck—in anger, in indecision. In, well, some bafflement as well, he was forced to admit. What was going on? What should he do about it?

He should go to bed, that's what. Let her come home when she was good and ready. She'd have much more to apologize for then, of course, but, well, *he* wasn't the one who'd stormed out of here like a rebellious teenager, was he?

He should get up, turn off the porch light, and go to bed.

Or should he leave it on? He didn't want to leave it burning all night, if she had checked into a hotel or something. What a stupid waste of electricity. It was the only light still on; a faint glow came through the small windows beside the door, growing lighter as his eyes adjusted to the dimness.

It still rankled, what Alicia had shouted at him in her hysteria. That "everyone" thought he was making a play for Steph, and that it was "making them all uncomfortable." What bull. It couldn't be true. They were just a group of friends, for god's sake. They got together every other week, and sometimes even more often—they all knew each other like family. He wouldn't...he hadn't...

You would, though, a small voice whispered in the back of his brain. The same voice that had steered his latest book project in such a bizarre direction. *You would do anything Steph was willing to do with you.*

But she's not willing, so that's that, he answered that voice. *Nothing to see here.*

He should go to bed.

I'm going to bed. I'm getting up now and going to bed.

Ron Alderson sat in the dark, in an empty house, before a cold fireplace.

~ o ~

READ ON FOR A SNEAK PEEK OF

The Touch of Silk

Book 3 in The Island of Second Chances

COMING SOON!

LYNNE

Lynne Daniels stood in the back room of the Evintrude Gallery, listening to the crowd on the other side of the door.

A huge crowd. A huge crowd here, tonight. A huge crowd here tonight for one reason: to see Lynne's tapestries, on display, on the walls and tables, *in an actual art gallery.*

Oh god.

Did this room have a fire exit?

The noise of the crowd increased as someone opened the door leading from the gallery's main room. Lynne froze. Kate Evintrude walked in, holding a glass of white wine, which she handed to Lynne. "Here, drink this, and no, you can't escape, so don't even think about it."

Lynne took the glass with a trembling hand. "How did you know?"

"Because the same thing happens with every artist, and not only on their first opening night. So drink up, take a deep breath, and come meet your adoring fans." Kate gave her a winning smile. "We've got a nice turnout."

Lynne moaned. "Why? *Why* are so many people here? Why did I agree to do this? What was I thinking? I'm a doctor, not an artist! I hate crowds!"

"Drink your wine."

Kate stared at Lynne until she took a sip. It was nice wine, dry, tart even, yet fruity—maybe grapefruity. "Is this Sauvignon Blanc?"

"It is. Drink some more."

Lynne obeyed. "From New Zealand?"

"Yep."

Kate watched as Lynne took several more sips.

"All right, that's probably enough," Kate said, when the glass was half-empty. "I think you're ready to head out there now."

"Oh god." Lynne looked behind her for that elusive—nonexistent—back door again. "I've changed my mind. I can't do this."

"I'll go out first and say a few words about your work and your life history, as we discussed," Kate said calmly, ignoring Lynne's panic attack. "You wait just inside the door, behind the screen, and as soon as I introduce you, you come out and give your little art talk. You have your notes, right?"

Lynne lifted up a folded sheet of paper. It had gotten a little creased and sweaty, but she thought she could still read what was on it.

"Great," Kate said, still exuding steady calmness. "Just say your piece, and then open it up for questions."

"Oh my god are people going to ask questions?"

Kate patted her arm. "Take another sip of wine. Of course they're going to ask questions, and you're going to answer them, because they're about your lovely and fascinating work, and people are going to want to hear all about it—from you."

"No they're not. No one wants to hear anything from me. I'm just an old woman who must have been drunk when some crazy gallery owner convinced her to hang her sewing mistakes on a wall for everyone to see."

"Hush now," Kate said. "Here we go." And she turned and stepped out of the back room and into the gallery, leaving Lynne alone. A moment later, Lynne heard her tapping a spoon on her own wine glass and calling for everyone's attention. The crowd slowly quieted.

And then Kate was talking about Lynne's work, and her life. How did she learn all those details? Did Steph tell her? Lynne couldn't remember talking to Kate about any of it.

Of course, Lynne couldn't remember a thing right now, her nervous brain freeze was so overwhelming.

But then Kate's spiel was over, and she called out Lynne's name, and the audience applauded!

As if sleepwalking, Lynne saw her feet move, and her feet were attached to her legs so they moved as well, carrying her out from behind the screen and into the gallery. My god, there were so many people here. *Don't think about them,* she told herself, as Kate smiled and indicated that Lynne should step up to the front table beside her. "Lynne Daniels, everyone!" Kate said, beaming at the crowd.

The applause redoubled, every single person smiling at Lynne. She smiled back at them, or at least she hoped it was a smile and not a rictus of terror.

And then the clapping died down and Lynne cleared her throat, unfolded her sheet of notes, and began her talk.

She must have gotten sucked into another dimension for a minute or ten, because suddenly she was done with her talk and slipping the crumpled paper into the pocket of her flowing pants, and the audience was smiling and applauding again, and then a dozen or more hands went up! People actually did have questions! Lynne looked over the crowd. Who to call on first? Why were there so many complete strangers here? Ah, there was Julie, from soup group. "Yes, Julie?" she said.

Julie smiled and said, "Your work is gorgeous, and so unusual; thank you for sharing it with us." Lynne nodded as Julie went on. "I was wondering, do you take commissions?"

"I, er, haven't before, but..." She looked at Kate, who took over smoothly.

"Lynne would be happy to talk to anyone about what they might have in mind," the gallery owner said. "Though she will make no promises—as I mentioned earlier, the artist Lynne Daniels is also the not-exactly-retired Doctor Lynne Daniels, as many of you know from encountering her at our health clinic." There were nods and smiles around the room. "More questions?"

All those hands went up again. Lynne scanned the crowd. "Yes?" she said, indicating a young woman in the back.

"Yes! Thank you, wow. I'm just getting into embroidery, and your work is *so* inspiring."

"Thank you," Lynne said.

The young woman nodded. "I've been working with floss, and not separating it, because I'm still figuring out how it all works, but I do know you can pull the threads apart for a finer line."

"That's correct."

"What I'm wondering is, how does that work with the various fabrics? I see that you do a lot of work on silk—which, first of all, oh my god. But also, isn't the weave of silk so tight for the thicker floss? How do you get both weights of thread to work together in the same piece—in the same *part* of the same piece?" She pointed to the landscape tapestry she was standing beside, a depiction of the West Sound harbor, at sunset.

Oh, what a good question. Lynne started talking as she walked over to the young woman, so she could point out the particulars of the piece. The crowd parted around her, watching and listening raptly. Her nerves melted away as she explained the process— how she'd stumbled across it by mistake during a moment of inattention, but found she really liked the effect, so she'd started doing it deliberately.

"I eventually had to rig up a larger hoop to keep the silk taut," Lynne finished, adding with a chuckle, "and it wasn't even hoop-shaped. My son helped with the construction." She looked up, finding Ethan's beaming face in the crowd. "Ethan Daniels, everyone."

The crowd applauded both her and Ethan; the young woman looked delighted. More hands went up, and Lynne found herself easily answering all their questions. Who knew so many people were interested in embroidery! It had always been something she'd done in the evenings alone at home, just to keep her hands busy while she watched TV or listened to an audiobook.

She had never thought of herself as an artist. Apparently, everyone else did.

After the tenth or twentieth question, there was another sound of a spoon tapping on a wine glass. "I'm going to stop us there," Kate called out, from the front table. "I'm sure Lynne will be happy to chat more with you individually throughout the evening, but we've got a buffet of great munchies ready to eat over by the far wall, and all this wine won't drink itself!"

Laughter filled the room, and conversations swelled as the audience moved toward the food and drink.

"Well?" Kate was suddenly beside her, smiling hugely, and handing her a fresh glass of wine. "How are you doing now?"

"Oh, that was amazing!" Lynne gushed, exulting in the adrenaline and the heavy relief of being off stage. "What a great crowd!"

"You were fantastic, as I knew you would be." Her tone was warm, and not at all smug; she really was just the nicest person. "And I've already had several very serious inquiries about purchasing pieces."

"That's great!" Lynne sipped the wine. "I really do need to make space in poor Ethan's room."

Kate laughed. "Yes, that's one reason why all this is a good idea, I suppose." Then she sobered a bit. "Are you certain you won't agree to sell the anchor piece, though?" She nodded to the long panorama of Crow Valley, stretching nearly the width of the gallery's eastern wall. "We would have a bidding war for it, just from the folks in this room."

"You know darn well it's already been sold, and for an absurdly generous price." Lynne looked through the audience again, and indeed, here came Steph—and her shy husband David! "I doubt you could talk her into letting it go, but you're welcome to try."

Kate pulled her friend Steph into a hug even as she said, "Leave it to you to snap up the best piece before the show even opened."

"There wouldn't even *be* a show if it weren't for my, ah, let's call it assistance," Steph said, laughing. She turned to Lynne. "So, now are you happy that we all pushed you into doing this?"

"Yes!" Lynne laughed with her. "Or at least I'm just so glad to be done with the public speaking part of the evening."

"How does a doctor have stage fright?" Steph asked. "Don't you have to give rounds and seminars, all the way from medical school onward? And you give a talk at the senior center here every week!"

"That's entirely different," Lynne said. "I can talk about medical things all day, to any size audience—I could do that in my sleep. Talking about my personal work…" She shrugged, and glanced at David, who was looking back at her with sympathy. "I know it's not rational, but I was waiting at any moment for someone to raise their hand and point out what an utter fraud I am."

"But that didn't happen," Kate said.

"Thank goodness!"

They all laughed as more people she knew made their way through the crowd. Julie and her boyfriend Gavin; Julie's daughter Megan; Matt; and…a vaguely familiar man.

After hugs and congratulations from her friends, Gavin indicated the silver-haired man beside him. "Lynne, you remember my friend Will?"

It took her a moment, but Will smiled and she placed him. "Oh! From pickleball last year—"

"—and beers afterwards," he finished, putting out a hand for her to shake. "It's a pleasure to see you again, and your work is spectacular."

"Thank you, and yes! I mean, the other way around—yes to the pleasure, and thank you for the compliment." She shook his hand; his grip was warm and strong, without crushing her smaller, more delicate hand. Indeed, her hand almost felt cradled, protected in the embrace of his. *What a strange thing to think!* she thought, only reluctantly letting go before the exchange became awkward—well, more awkward. *I must be completely wound up tonight.* "You look different in real clothes," she blurted, before she could stop herself. *Oops. More awkward, coming right up!*

Will laughed, looking down at himself. He was in what might be called cocktail-casual: dark slacks, a striped blue button-down shirt, no tie; his shirtsleeves were unbuttoned and turned up at the cuffs, exposing his tanned wrists. "Well, one doesn't wear sweatpants and a ball cap to an art opening, even on casual Orcas Island."

Lynne wanted to cover her mouth with her hand. *What is the matter with me?* She forced herself to laugh along with him as she glanced at her own outfit. "I thought the same. And now I should probably get something to eat before I make an even bigger fool of myself." She held up her glass of wine, which was more than half gone already.

"May I escort you over to the buffet?" Will asked, offering an elbow. Somehow, he made the gesture seem gallant and comfortable rather than stuffy or old-fashioned.

"Yes, thank you," Lynne said, and took his arm.

"We'll come too," Steph said, taking David's hand and following along. "I love other people's cooking."

"I don't know why that always surprises me," Julie observed.

Their whole little group moved toward the food, eventually securing plates of nibbles—cheese, rolled meats, crackers, olives. Then, somehow, she found herself standing with Will under the Crow Valley panorama.

"I inquired about purchasing this piece," Will said, "but Kate told me that it has already sold."

"It has," Lynne said. "To Steph—" She turned, looking for her friend, but she and David had vanished into the crowd. As had Matt, and Julie and Megan and Gavin, and Kate. "The redheaded woman who was with us earlier."

Will smiled. She hadn't remembered how good-looking he was. In fact, she'd barely remembered him at all; it had been a pleasant afternoon with friends, and that had been that. "Well, then, I suppose I'll need to be one of the people talking to you about a commission."

Lynne felt her face flush with warmth. "I...we would have to talk about that," she said. "I don't usually know, when I start a piece, where it will end up."

"I am comfortable with uncertainty." His smile grew even warmer.

Are we still talking about my needlework?

"Ah, good," she managed. "Well, uh..."

"Hey Mom!" Suddenly Ethan was at her elbow. "You wanna introduce me to your friend?"

"I'm Will Hamilton," Will said, putting out that wonderful strong hand. Ethan shook it.

"This is my son, Ethan," Lynne said.

"It's a pleasure to meet you," Will told him.

Ethan grinned. "Likewise!" He turned to Lynne. "Marie and I are going to head on out—we have that dinner, remember."

"That's right," Lynne said. "Well, thank you for being here for the opening."

"We wouldn't have missed it!"

She pulled her son into a hug. He took the opportunity to whisper in her ear, "Hubba hubba!"

"Stop it," she hissed back to him, though she couldn't help laughing as well as she let him go. "Have fun this evening!" she said brightly, and glanced around for Marie.

"She's already getting the car," Ethan told her. "We had to park, like, blocks and blocks away. This place is packed tonight!"

Lynne didn't point out that all of Eastsound barely comprised "blocks and blocks."

After he'd left, she turned back to Will, who was studying the tapestry. "You do have a singular talent," he said.

"This entire experience is going to go completely to my head and I will become quite insufferable," Lynne protested. "It's just threads on fabric!"

Will turned and held her gaze. His eyes were a rich, warm brown shot through with green flecks of an almost jade-like brightness, picking up the silver of his hair and his neatly trimmed beard. Lynne didn't usually like men with beards, but this one... She found herself unable to look away from him, and also, automatically, thinking about how she would depict that play of colors in a piece. "Oh, I don't think so," he said. "It is so much more than that."

The rest of the crowded, noisy room seemed to fall away as she stared into his eyes.

"In fact," Will went on, "I would be honored to buy you dinner and continue this conversation in a quieter venue."

Lynne swallowed. "I would like that," she said.

Notes and Thanks

As I mentioned at the end of *A Taste of Midnight*, book 1 of the Island of Second Chances (aka "the Sunday Soup Group books"), authors don't always get to decide which books they write...sometimes the characters in our heads simply demand to have their stories told. I couldn't very well leave Steph and David hanging right after I sent him back to Steph's bed, could I?

And so, out came another Sunday Soup Group book.

A reminder, from book 1: This series is set on Orcas Island, but it's an Orcas that's not entirely contiguous with the one we know out here in the real world. There are real businesses in the books, and then there are made-up ones. I played with some geography for the sake of making the story work. And, of course, so far as I know, there are no plans in the works for parking meters.

Thanks again go to Kathia Zolfaghari for the simply splendid cover, and to Spencer Ellsworth for his absolutely spot-on editing—yes, this book *also* gained ten thousand words after he went through it. Thanks to Didier Gincig of the Orcas Island Odd Fellows Hall for the cheerful help and information. Thanks *always* to Darvill's Bookstore for their eternal love and support!

And thank *you*, dear reader, for joining me on another fictional journey!

Shannon Page
May, 2025
Orcas Island, Washington

ABOUT THE AUTHOR

SHANNON PAGE LIVES on Orcas Island, with her husband, author and illustrator Mark Ferrari. The island is an amazing place to live, and to write. She's a versatile writer (which sounds much better than saying she can't make up her mind!), publishing novels of fantasy, cozy mystery, romance, and science fiction, as well as personal essays; for her "day job," she's a freelance proofreader and copy editor. She also loves to edit anthologies. In her spare time (haha), she cooks, gardens, plays pickleball, and takes *lots* of pictures of frogs. Visit her at www.shannonpage.net.